Broken Trail

Jean Rae Baxter

RONSDALE PRESS

RONSDALE PRESS
3350 West 21st Avenue, Vancouver, B.C., Canada V6S 1G7
www.ronsdalepress.com

Typesetting: Julie Cochrane, in Minion 12 pt on 16
Cover Art & Design: Nancy de Brouwer, Massive Graphic
Paper: Ancient Forest Friendly "Silva" (FSC) — 100% post-consumer waste, totally chlorine-free and acid-free

Ronsdale Press wishes to thank the following for their support of its publishing program: the Canada Council for the Arts, the Government of Canada through the Canada Book Program, the British Columbia Arts Council, and the Province of British Columbia through the British Columbia Book Publishing Tax Credit program.

Library and Archives Canada Cataloguing in Publication

Baxter, Jean Rae, 1932–
Broken trail / Jean Rae Baxter.

ISBN 978-1-55380-109-2

I. Title.

PS8603.A935B76 2011 jC813'.6 C2010-904456-8

At Ronsdale Press we are committed to protecting the environment. To this end we are working with Canopy (formerly Markets Initiative) and printers to phase out our use of paper produced from ancient forests. This book is one step towards that goal.

Printed in Canada by Marquis Printing, Quebec

BROKEN TRAIL

OTHER WORKS BY
JEAN RAE BAXTER

A Twist of Malice
Seraphim Editions, 2005

The Way Lies North
Ronsdale Press, 2007

Looking for Cardenio
Seraphim Editions, 2008

to my grandchildren,
with love:

Trevor, Riley, Patrick,
Karen, Nathan, Jay,
Naomi and Thomas

ACKNOWLEDGEMENTS

My main source for information about Patrick Ferguson is Dr. M. M. Gilchrist's *Patrick Ferguson: "A Man of Some Genius"* (Edinburgh: NMS Publications, 2003). My thanks to Gretchen Runnalls for putting me in touch with Professor Gilchrist. I am also indebted to *The Indian How Book* by Arthur C. Parker [Gawaso Wanneh] (New York: Doubleday, Doran & Company, 1941) and to the *Diary of Lieutenant Anthony Allaire*, of the Loyal American Regiment, assigned to the command of Major Patrick Ferguson. Out of respect for Dr. Gilchrist and other scholars whose work I have consulted, I must emphasize that any historical inaccuracies are my responsibility and mine only.

I am especially grateful to Ronald B. Hatch for his perseverance in guiding my manuscript through its various drafts and for pointing the way that my journey ought to go. My thanks, also, to Erinna Gilkison for her skill in ferreting out flaws and adding a final polish to the story. A big thank you to Thomas Baxter for reading the first draft. I am also grateful to Janet Myers and to Karen Baxter for their helpful suggestions. Thanks are due, as always, to my friends in the Creative Writing Group of the Canadian Federation of University Women (Hamilton Branch) for their valuable comments on particular scenes. Finally, my love and gratitude to my daughter, Alison Baxter Lean, whose natural affection has not dulled the edge of her keen legal mind. I especially appreciate her honesty in identifying weaknesses and suggesting ways my writing can be made better.

Prologue

JUNE 1779

AFTER MANY DAYS on the trail, it was good to return to the village. There was meat to share and there were skins for the women to clean and make soft. Broken Trail had killed a deer, not just rabbits and grouse like the other boys in the hunting party.

His uncle, Carries a Quiver, stood in the centre of the dancing circle, with everyone watching, and made the boast, "It was Broken Trail's arrow that brought down this deer. He is a hunter who brings meat for the people."

Broken Trail had trouble keeping a straight face when he saw the scowl on Walks Crooked's face. Let him scowl! He was angry because it was not his clumsy son Spotted Dog who had killed the deer. Walks Crooked's anger made the triumph sweeter still, for his voice was the loudest among those denying Broken Trail's fitness to be a warrior. Now Broken Trail had proved him wrong, for everyone knew that a boy who killed his first deer at eleven years old was destined to become a mighty hunter.

The women were dragging away the deer to butcher when Black Elk approached.

"We have been waiting for your return," Black Elk said. "We have taken a captive. A white girl. She speaks only English. We want to question her."

This news dulled the edge of Broken Trail's joy. Although his command of English made him valued as an interpreter, he hated any reminder of where he came from.

"Where is she?"

"You will find her in Wolf Woman's lodge."

"Wolf Woman is old and weak. How can she guard a captive?"

"The girl needs a healer, not a guard. Our warriors found her lying injured on the side of a steep ravine. She appeared to have fallen over the edge, and a tree stopped her from tumbling all the way. We want you to speak with her before we question her. Win her trust."

Broken Trail looked down and shuffled his feet. He didn't want to talk to the white girl.

Black Elk continued. "Tell her that we shall not harm her. Say nothing more. The elders will decide what to do with her. I will take you to her now."

The girl was sitting on a log just outside the entrance of Wolf Woman's lodge. She wore a fringed, beaded doeskin poncho over a short leather skirt. Her dark hair hung in two braids, with a red stripe painted along the centre part. In every respect except the colour of her skin, she looked like an Oneida maiden. Yet Broken Trail recognized her at once. This was Charlotte Hooper, the girl who had befriended him two years ago when he and his first mother and his brother and baby sister had camped by Oneida Lake during their journey north to the safety of a British fort. That was before he ran away.

The girl did not notice their approach. She was staring off into the woods, toward a clump of alder bushes, as if her thoughts were miles away. Black Elk and Broken Trail were standing right in front of her before she turned her head to face them. Her eyes widened as she stared at Broken Trail.

"I remember you." Her voice was barely audible under her breath. "You are Moses Cobman."

The name hurt, like an insult or a taunt. "No longer. My name is Broken Trail."

He kept his face rigid, as a warrior should. After they had stared at each other for a few moments, she stated firmly, "But you're Moses Cobman all the same."

She had no right to speak to him like that. He turned his back on her and stalked away.

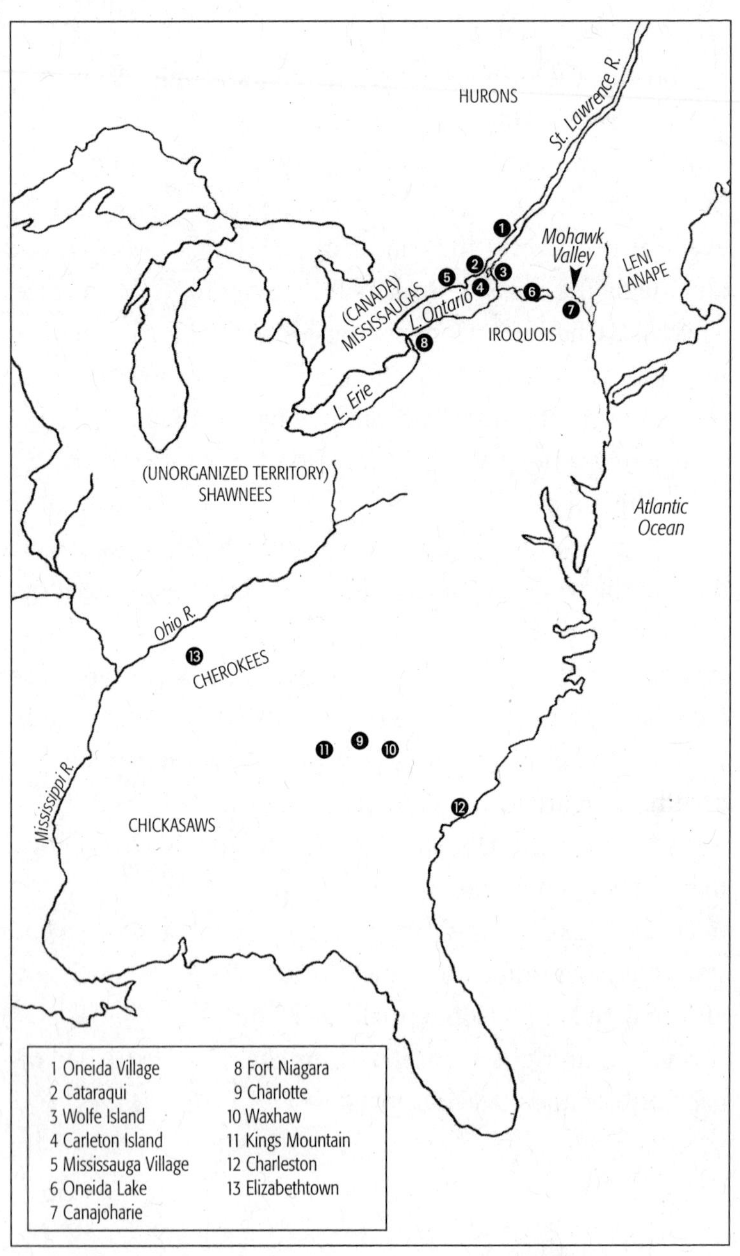
HURONS
St. Lawrence R.
Mohawk Valley
LENI LANAPE
(CANADA) MISSISSAUGAS
L. Ontario
IROQUOIS
L. Erie
(UNORGANIZED TERRITORY) SHAWNEES
Atlantic Ocean
Ohio R.
CHEROKEES
Mississippi R.
CHICKASAWS
1 Oneida Village
2 Cataraqui
3 Wolfe Island
4 Carleton Island
5 Mississauga Village
6 Oneida Lake
7 Canajoharie
8 Fort Niagara
9 Charlotte
10 Waxhaw
11 Kings Mountain
12 Charleston
13 Elizabethtown

Chapter 1

SEPTEMBER 1780

FOR TEN DAYS BROKEN TRAIL had fasted in the wilderness. Only water had entered his mouth. He had chanted. He had prayed with all his soul to see his totem animal, his *oki*, who would be his protector throughout life. He had opened his heart to the whisperings of the unseen spirits and his eyes to the vision he would behold.

Broken Trail had completed all the rites of purification, bathed in cleansing water into which boiled leaves and ferns had been mixed, swallowed bitter emetics to remove every bit of waste. Body and soul, he was clean. His uncle, Carries a Quiver, had assured him that he would be acceptable to the Great Spirit, even though white by birth. And his uncle was the wisest man he knew.

Then why had no vision come to him? The only whispering he heard was the wind in the tall trees. The closest thing to a vision was a shower of falling stars. But that often happened in late summer, when the stars shook loose in the sky.

His friend Young Bear had fasted nine days before his vision came. His *oki* was an osprey. After the osprey had spoken to him, the spirits revealed a glimpse of Young Bear's former life, when he had been a chief among faraway people who hollowed their boats from logs. His vision had also foretold his heroic death in battle. It was good to know these things. At thirteen, Young Bear had already made up his death song, to be ready in case his first war party should be his last.

What if Broken Trail's vision should fail? He tried not to think about that. Ten days was a long time, yet he knew that some waited even longer before their vision finally came to them. It was rare for no *oki* to appear, but it did happen. The man who dug the village garbage holes had failed to receive a vision, so of course he could not be a warrior.

Broken Trail stood up and stretched. He had spent the entire morning sitting under an ash tree beside a creek, doing nothing but waiting and praying. His body was weak with hunger, but he must not eat until his *oki* appeared to him. Maybe he would not feel quite so famished if he filled his stomach with water. A few steps away, there was a quiet pool at a bend in the creek.

As Broken Trail leaned over the edge of the pool, a water

spider swam through his reflection. He studied the face that looked up at him. Brown hair, blue eyes, skin bronzed by the sun yet paler than the skin of his friends. I look like Elijah, he thought, before immediately trying to drive the thought from his mind.

Broken Trail imagined that he could hear Elijah's voice and feel his hand upon his shoulder. "I'll take you hunting," Elijah had said. But he never did. All white men were liars.

I must not think about him, Broken Trail told himself. He plunged his hands into the water, and the reflection vanished. Lifting his cupped hands to his mouth, he drank the cool, fresh water. Then he stood up, raised his face to the sky and chanted the prayer that Carries a Quiver had taught him:

O Great Spirit, my heart is open.
Let my *oki* come to me.
Let me see his visible form.
Let him promise me his protection.
My heart is open, O Great Spirit.
Show me a vision of my future.
Show me the path that lies ahead.

As he finished the prayer, his heart felt suddenly light, and his head as well. A dizzy sensation came over him, but he forced himself to stay on his feet.

"I'm ready," he said. "Let my vision come to me."

As if summoned, a wolverine walked out of the bushes

and stood looking at him—the biggest wolverine he had ever seen. It had the shape of a bear and the size of a wolf. Its shaggy fur was dark brown, with two broad yellowish bands, one on each side, reaching backward from the shoulder to meet at the base of its tail. Broken Trail smelled its pungent musk. The wolverine looked at him sideways. Opening its mouth, it showed Broken Trail its sharp yellow teeth.

Broken Trail waited, afraid to speak lest he offend it.

It spoke to him in thoughts, not words, so that he heard its message not with his ears but with his mind. "Broken Trail, I am your *oki*, come to protect you from all harm. Hear what I say, and remember well."

"I will," the boy whispered.

At that instant, a rifle cracked. Within the rush of noise, Broken Trail felt a sharp pain in his right thigh. He grabbed at his leg, but his eyes were still on the wolverine as it raised its head, turned aside, and loped into the forest.

As he watched it disappear into the undergrowth, Broken Trail tried to call out, to summon it back. No sound came from his lips. His mind was numb with disbelief. At the very moment of revelation, he had been shot, and his *oki* had run away.

Broken Trail felt his knees give way. For a moment his eyes were still directed toward the spot where the wolverine had slipped away. Then the pain of his wound forced him to look down at the red stain spreading around the hole in his legging where the bullet had entered. He felt wetness run down his leg.

Should he go back to the village? He took one step, and then another. Despite the pain, he could walk. But he was not sure what he wanted to do. If he returned home, he would have to tell his uncle that his *oki* had gone away before revealing his destiny. Had such a thing ever happened before? It might be a terrible omen. Yet the wolverine had appeared to him, and it had spoken. His vision had not completely failed. If the elders believed more was needed, maybe they would let him try again.

Through the turmoil of his mind came the crashing sound of men's boots. White men.

Someone shouted, "You got him, Frank. We'll find the brute and finish him off."

Broken Trail flinched. Better slide into a thicket where they would not see him. But before he could hide, two men burst through the undergrowth. Redcoats. Each carried a rifle. Both looked ready to fire.

When they saw Broken Trail, they lowered their guns. They stared at him. He drove the pain from his expression to return their stares. They were young men. One was tall and thin, with fair hair pulled back in a queue. The other was short and sturdily built, with black hair.

The short soldier laughed. "Frank, that's not a wolverine."

"No. God forgive me. I aimed at a wolverine, but I shot a boy. He's hurt. Sam, what are we going to do?"

"We'd better see how bad he's hurt."

Broken Trail felt his body swaying. In a moment, he would faint like a girl.

"Hey, there!" The tall soldier grabbed one arm, and the short soldier took the other. Broken Trail tried to shake them off, but they had a firm grip. When they had him sitting down, Frank undid the thong that attached Broken Trail's right legging to his belt. He pulled down the top of the legging.

"Not too bad." Sam gently touched the area around the wound. "The bullet passed in and out. A flesh wound. He's lucky it never touched bone."

"But he's bleeding, and he's looking mighty weak. We'd best take him back to camp so the surgeon can bandage that leg. I shot him. I can't just leave him here."

"No!" Broken Trail blurted.

"Hey!" Frank exclaimed. "The little savage speaks English."

Broken Trail looked up. Two pairs of blue eyes met.

"You're no Indian," Frank said slowly. "You're as white as me."

Broken Trail decided not to say another word.

"There's a mystery here," Sam said. "Captain will want to meet this boy."

Chapter 2

WHAT A STRANGE DAY this had been! And it was not over yet. First, his *oki* had appeared to him. But before it could show him a vision of his future, the crack of a rifle had driven it away. At the same moment, a bullet had struck his thigh. He had only a hazy recollection of what had happened next. Two soldiers had carried him to an army camp. The surgeon, an officer wearing a smock over his uniform, had bandaged his thigh. Broken Trail touched the bandage with his fingers. Yes, this really had happened.

And now he was lying on a narrow cot in a tent, wondering what would happen next. Clearly visible against the white canvas was the shadow of a soldier standing outside the entrance, holding a musket. Broken Trail could think of no reason why he should be under guard. It must have something to do with the captain who the soldier had said would want to meet him. But why? Because he was white? He had heard of captives who had been adopted by Indians being forcibly returned to their white families. If anybody did that to him, he'd run away again.

Maybe he ought to run away right now. From where he lay, he could see his tomahawk, his sheathed knife, his pouch, his leggings and his moccasins neatly piled on the tent floor. One legging and one moccasin were spattered with blood.

All he had to do was rise from the cot, put on his leggings and moccasins, assemble his other possessions, and make a dash for it. If he was fast enough, he should be able to escape the guard standing outside the tent.

Sitting up carefully, Broken Trail swung both legs over the side of the cot. He stood. He took two steps. Despite a sharp twinge, his right leg worked as well as his left. Four more steps brought him to the pile of his possessions. When he stooped to gather them up, a wave of dizziness swept over him. He knew what it meant; ten days' fasting had taken away his strength. He was too weak to go anywhere without first having something to eat.

The world seemed to be tilting and shifting as he staggered back to the cot. For several moments he sat still, waiting for his head to stop spinning. Then he put on his leggings and moccasins, attached the various items to his belt, and lay down again.

Someone was coming. A second shadow moved against the white canvas. The tent flap opened, and a redcoat entered. It was the tall soldier, Frank, carrying a tin bowl and a spoon.

"Here's your vittles," he said, setting the bowl and spoon on the small folding table that stood beside the cot. "Hope you're feeling better."

The soldier stood awkwardly for a few moments, shifting from one foot to the other and looking as if he were waiting for Broken Trail to say something. But Broken Trail, who had no intention of speaking to him, turned his face away and scowled.

"Well, good luck to you, anyway," the soldier said. "You know I meant no harm."

Broken Trail waited until the soldier had left before sitting up to grab the bowl and spoon. He inspected the bowl's contents. White man's food. Pork and beans simmered with molasses. He lowered his nose and sniffed. Hmm! The rich aroma made his mouth water. Long ago, pork and beans had been his favourite meal.

As he gulped down the food, his white mother's face arose before him and he could not drive the memory of a warm farm kitchen from his mind.

He had finished eating before two other redcoats entered the tent. These were men he had not seen before. One was a young officer with a stubby, turned-up nose. He carried a writing tablet. The other was a senior officer, a thin erect man wearing a white periwig. This must be the captain whom Broken Trail had heard about. He was glad that the

British had him, not the rebels, for it was the rebels who had driven his people from their land. Yet it made little difference. He hated both.

Broken Trail scrambled off the cot. To be lying down while the captain questioned him would make him look weak. Now that he had food in his belly, his legs were steady and his mind was clear.

"So you speak English?" the captain said, with no words of greeting or introduction.

Broken Trail nodded.

"We know you're white. The thing we don't know is what you're doing here in the bush, dressed like a wild Indian."

Broken Trail shrugged.

"What's your name?"

Broken Trail hesitated. The redcoats knew he spoke English. There was no point pretending that he didn't. He did not know why the captain was asking him questions. But if he co-operated, maybe they would let him go sooner.

"Broken Trail," he said.

"Your real name."

"It is my real name."

"Have you ever had a different name? Or don't you remember?"

"Moses Cobman," he muttered.

"Where were you born?"

"Canajoharie, in the Mohawk Valley."

The young officer's eyes widened. "Sir," he exclaimed. "I

know who this boy is. While we were stationed at Fort Niagara, our regiment shared quarters with the Royal Greens. There was a private called Elijah Cobman who came from Canajoharie. He told us that Oneida Indians carried off his youngest brother three years ago."

Startled, Broken Trail looked up at the young officer. For the first time in three years, he had heard someone say Elijah's name.

"Canajoharie! Is that so?" The captain looked intently at Broken Trail. "Does your family still live there?"

Broken Trail shook his head. "My father and my oldest brother joined Butler's Rangers. They were off fighting rebels when some neighbours burned our house. That's when we left Canajoharie and headed north."

"So all your family are Loyalists?"

"I reckon so." It would be pointless to explain that those people were no longer his family.

"How old are you?"

"Nearly thirteen."

"Well, you're small for your age, but old enough." He fixed his pale blue eyes on Broken Trail. "What I need is a courier, a man with experience in delivering messages between forts and to armies in the field, someone who can survive in the bush, ford rivers, and cross mountain ranges without getting lost. But we're short of couriers. When the rebels capture one, they don't treat him as a prisoner of war. They hang him from the nearest tree."

Broken Trail waited for the captain to make his point.

"I thought of using one of my own men," the captain continued, "but there isn't a single soldier in this company who has the skills that are needed." He paused. "Of course, an Indian could do it. But Indians aren't reliable."

Not reliable! Broken Trail clenched his fists. He would trust a brother Oneida long before he would trust any white man.

"But you're different," the captain went on to say. "You're born white. You speak English. And you have your father and two brothers fighting for the King. Isn't that right?"

"Yes."

The captain continued, "I'll take a chance on you. If you can carry a message to Kings Mountain in twelve days, you'll get a new flintlock rifle for your pains."

A rifle! Now the captain had captured his full attention. There was nothing he yearned for as much as a rifle. If he owned a rifle, he was bound to become the best hunter in the whole Oneida nation. Walks Crooked and Spotted Dog would burn with envy.

"Where is Kings Mountain? I never heard of it." Broken Trail kept his face rigid, not letting his excitement show.

"South Carolina."

"I never heard of it either."

"It's down south, through the mountains, a long way from here."

"I'll think about it. But I can't go on a long trail right now.

First, I have to go back to my village. There's something important I must tell my uncle."

"No time to spare. Tell him afterwards, when you have your new rifle to show off. You'll spend the night here, then start off at dawn."

Broken Trail hesitated. Would it be right to leave on a long trail without telling Carries a Quiver about the wolverine? He looked down at his feet, then up at the ridgepole, and finally at the captain's white periwig. Well, what difference would it make if he delivered the message first? When he told the people of his village that he had been all the way through the mountains on an important mission, and had a new rifle to prove it, who then could doubt his fitness to be a warrior?

"This place, Kings Mountain, who lives there?"

"It's Cherokee territory—Indians live there, and settlers known as Over Mountain men. I don't know which are more dangerous, the red savages or the white." His eyes studied Broken Trail's face. "Most of the way is through mountains. You can go over the mountains or follow the river valleys. Climbing cuts the distance in half." He fixed Broken Trail with his cold blue eyes. Broken Trail broke the silence.

"I'll need food to carry with me."

The moment he said this, Broken Trail knew that he would go. This was not a conscious decision, but a feeling that he must, although he had no idea why. This mission was something that belonged to him, just as his *oki* belonged to him. This was different from the way in which the rifle would belong to him—it was much more special than that.

"We'll supply you with food. What else do you need, a boy like you?"

His eyes ran over Broken Trail's new moccasins of smoked buckskin, his doeskin shirt, his leather leggings with designs worked in porcupine quills, and his belt. Especially his belt, for in it Broken Trail wore his tomahawk; and from his belt hung his precious knife in its decorated sheath and his pouch that held bits of sinew for sewing, fishing line, bone fish hooks and the thong he used to rig up a fire-bow when on the trail.

"I need a gun."

The captain chuckled. "No, my boy. You'll get the gun after you deliver the message. If I gave it to you now, you and the gun would both be gone for good." He turned to the young officer. "Cornet, fetch this boy some hardtack."

The young officer left the tent.

"What's the message you want me to carry?"

"That doesn't concern you."

"I reckon it does, if I'm about to risk my life."

The captain laughed. It was a short, dry laugh. "You're a bold lad. Well, here's the gist of it. We have an army on the march from Virginia, one thousand Loyalist troops—we call them the Loyal Americans—heading west."

"Any Royal Greens with them?"

"Uh, yes, I believe so." He cleared his throat. "As I was

about to say, their commander, Major Patrick Ferguson, is an experienced military man. However, he made a rash boast that has put his whole army at risk. He sent a message to the Over Mountain men, threatening to march his army over the mountains, hang their leaders and lay their country waste with fire and sword unless they stopped helping the rebels."

To Broken Trail such a boast sounded reasonable. Among the Oneida, boasting was part of the preparation for battle. Warriors boasted about how many enemies they would kill and how many scalps they would take.

The captain continued: "Major Ferguson is a Scot from Edinburgh. He's a brilliant man, but he doesn't know a damn thing about those Over Mountain men." He laughed again, that sharp humourless laugh. "Did you ever hit a hornets' nest with a stick?"

"Just once."

"Exactly. Over Mountain men from every county west of Blue Ridge came swarming out hot as hornets. By reputation, they're great marksmen. No military training. No uniforms or provisions. No expectation of pay, so far as anybody knows, yet they've raised a militia force over one thousand strong. Just yesterday I received a report that they plan to rendezvous in the Watauga Valley on September 25th."

"When is that? I haven't seen a calendar in three years."

"Day after tomorrow. After that, they'll need about ten days to get organized for a march into the mountains, where they plan to join forces with about three hundred and fifty militiamen from other counties. They're bent on one thing and one thing only—to wipe out Major Ferguson and all his men."

"So you want me to warn Major Ferguson?"

"Correct. Ferguson doesn't know how to fight in the mountains. If he doesn't withdraw to Charleston, his army will be cut to pieces." The captain unrolled a map and placed it on the table. "Here's where you're to go. Kings Mountain, South Carolina." He rested one finger upon the intended spot. Broken Trail had never before seen such clean fingernails, such smooth well-tended hands. "After we ferry you across the St. Lawrence, you head south. When you get to Oneida Lake, go around the west end."

"I know where that is." He had been only nine years old, but how could he forget that place? The day he ran away, the warriors who found him led him to their band's fishing village at the west end of the lake. They took away his shirt, his breeches and his boots. They dressed him in a leather tunic, leggings and moccasins. Oneida Lake was where his new life had begun.

"Fine. From the west end of the lake, you travel southeast. You won't have much trouble until you reach the mountains in Pennsylvania. From that point, there'll be mountains all the way." The captain reached up with both hands and adjusted his periwig, which had begun to slide towards his nose. "Have you ever heard of Charlotte?"

Charlotte! Broken Trail winced. Not her again!

"I know a girl named Charlotte."

"Well, you certainly do get around!" The captain snorted. "The Charlotte I have in mind is a town twenty-five miles east of Kings Mountain."

Broken Trail scratched his head. "Oneida Lake is as far south as I've ever been."

"Do you think you'll lose your way?"

"Not so long as sunrise and sunset stay where they belong. Besides, I can ask."

"That's what I'm counting on. You can travel like an Indian but talk like a white man."

The young officer re-entered the tent, carrying a small canvas bag with a drawstring top.

"Here's hardtack." He handed the bag to Broken Trail. "A little goes a long way."

Broken Trail peered into the bag. Its contents were pale, hard biscuits that looked about as appetizing as wood chips. He looped the bag's drawstring onto his belt.

"Now," said the captain, "here's the message you're to deliver to Major Ferguson." He gave Broken Trail a folded sheet of paper. "Don't give it to anyone else. That's the only way you can be sure it reaches his hands."

"How will I know who he is? What does he look like?"

"Small in stature. He has brown hair, which he wears powdered. On the battlefield he stands out because he wears a checkered hunting shirt over his uniform, rides a grey horse, and gives orders by blowing a silver whistle. However, he won't be on the battlefield when you see him. Ask a sentry to direct you to his tent."

Broken Trail started to unfold the paper.

"Hold on there," the captain said. "No reason for you to look at that. Just keep it safe."

"I want to know where it says, 'Give this boy a rifle.'"

"Smart lad." The captain took back the paper and, without unfolding it, took the charcoal pencil that the young officer had been using and hastily wrote a few words. He handed it to Broken Trail. "I'm surprised that you can read."

"I had three years of schooling." Broken Trail studied the note. He read aloud, 'If this reaches you, give the bear a rifle for his trouble.'" He frowned. "What's this about a bear?"

"That's you," the captain laughed his short, sharp laugh. "The word I wrote is 'bearer,' not 'bear.' You should have stayed in school a while longer."

Chapter 3

IT WAS HARD TO RELAX on the narrow army cot, especially with so many thoughts whirling in his head. Twelve days to deliver the message. The journey would be long. Beyond the wrecked fishing village at the western end of Oneida Lake, Broken Trail knew no landmarks by which to measure his progress toward Kings Mountain.

All he could do, he thought, was travel as fast as possible. The sooner he delivered the message, the sooner he could return home. He did not care about the fate of Major Ferguson and his Loyal Americans, but for a rifle he would do his best.

Only once in his life had he ever had a chance to fire a

gun. The warrior Swift Fox, his uncle's friend, had owned an old muzzle-loading musket picked up from a battlefield twenty winters ago, in the days when the Oneida nation had helped the English against the French. When Broken Trail was eleven, Swift Fox had let him try to shoot with it. The noise had deafened his ear, and the kick had knocked him off his feet. Such a gun was not the stuff of his dreams.

He admired the new breech-loading rifles that several Oneida warriors had bought from traders. Not only were these weapons lighter and more accurate than a musket, but a warrior could reload while lying under a bush. Among boys his age, only Spotted Dog owned such a rifle—a gift to celebrate his mystic vision. If Broken Trail delivered his message in time, maybe Major Ferguson would give him a gun like that.

In the moments before sleep, Broken Trail imagined the rifle that would soon be his.

A bugle's blare woke him at dawn. Broken Trail blinked up at the ridgepole of the tent. He barely had time to focus his thoughts before a soldier entered, carrying another bowl of pork and beans. This soldier was older than the two who had brought him to the army camp.

He waited until Broken Trail sat up before handing him the bowl. Instead of leaving the tent, he watched from under the brim of his forage cap while Broken Trail picked up the spoon and took his first mouthful.

"So you're the boy who's taking a message to the great Pat

Ferguson. He's a man I long to meet. I envy you, though I reckon you won't have much chance to talk with him."

"Reckon not." Broken Trail shovelled another spoonful of beans into his mouth.

"Ferguson's designed a new kind of rifle. They say it's five times more accurate than an old firelock. There's talk the light infantry will be outfitted with Ferguson rifles. If that happens, we still might win the war." He heaved a sigh. "Not likely, more's the pity." Then he clamped his mouth shut, as if realizing too late that he should not be talking like this, even to a boy.

But a moment later he started up again. "The officers don't tell us anything. But we men think this company is about to be sent down south. That's where the real fighting is going on. Virginia. The Carolinas. Georgia. With luck, I still might end up under Major Ferguson's command."

Broken Trail, busily scraping the bottom of the bowl, did not answer. When he had finished the last spoonful, he set down the bowl on the folding table.

"I'm ready."

"The canoe's waiting. It's time to be off."

Fog shrouded the river. Broken Trail, sitting in the middle of the canoe, saw only whiteness all around. Nor was there anything to hear, apart from the dripping of water from the paddles.

As the sun burned off the fog, dozens of islands came into

view. Some were large and wooded, and others just a rock with a single gnarled tree clinging by its roots. The canoe wove among them on its way to the St. Lawrence River's south bank.

On one island he saw an osprey's nest, a rough platform of sticks balanced at the top of a dead pine. His friend Young Bear's *oki* was an osprey. If Young Bear were with him now, Broken Trail would tell him about the wolverine. A wolverine must be the equal of an osprey. It was larger and fiercer, though maybe not as noble.

Young Bear was slightly older than Broken Trail. He had completed his dream quest in the spring, three moons ago. Now he was entitled to wear his hair like a warrior, with a scalp lock into which was woven a decoration of bright beads. No trophy feathers yet. Ready for his first war party, he had been waiting all summer for Broken Trail to catch up.

Broken Trail wondered what his friend was doing right now. He might be checking his snares. He might still be asleep on his bearskin on his family's sleeping platform in the longhouse. If awake, he might be thinking about Broken Trail, worried that something bad had happened to him. Eleven days had passed since his dream quest began. That was a long time.

The backward churning of the stern paddle roused Broken Trail. The canoe had reached the far side of the river. The paddlers held the canoe steady while he climbed out onto the bank.

With a brief, "Good luck," the soldiers backed up the canoe and turned it around. Broken Trail watched their departure. After a moment he turned away and, with the sunrise on his left, began to walk.

The path led through leafy woods, their green tinged with scarlet and gold; then there was a stretch of low scrub, followed by more woods. Broken Trail kept to an easy pace that would not cause his wound to start bleeding again.

Around midday, when he began to feel hungry, he pulled a hardtack biscuit from the bag. He nibbled one corner. The biscuit had no flavour at all. But his stomach rumbled, and he had nothing else to eat. Broken Trail broke off a piece and, as he walked along, managed to chew it into a doughy paste that he could swallow.

Toward evening, he came to a green glade with a stream running through it. Here he stopped to make camp for the night. Taking off his blood-stiffened legging, he washed it in the stream and laid it over a bush to dry. The bandage on his right thigh looked clean. No fresh bleeding. Tomorrow, he thought, he would be able to walk faster.

Blueberries were plentiful in the glade, tiny dusky globes bursting with sweetness. He feasted on berries and then lay down on a bed of spruce boughs, not bothering to make a fire. It was a warm night. The chirping of a thousand crickets kept him company, and he slept well.

In the morning his right leg was stiff, although the stiffness eased once he started moving. Again, he chewed hardtack as he walked along. The wet leather of the legging he had washed felt clammy against his skin. But soon he ceased to notice, and by the end of the day it was dry.

That evening he removed the bandage from his thigh. The wound was healing well. There would be a small scar—something to remind him of the day his *oki* revealed itself to him.

On the third day of his journey he reached the west end of Oneida Lake. Charred poles poking up through the grass were all that remained of the fishing village that had stood here three years ago. This was the place to which the warriors who found him in the woods had brought him, a runaway child discovered sleeping in a pile of leaves. He remembered his first impression of the people's dark faces and the mingled smells of smoke and fish. From that day, he had felt at home among them.

He would stop here for the night, he decided. And he would fish for his supper. No need to eat hardtack when Oneida Lake teemed with fish. Almost as soon as he threw his line into the water, a big pickerel took the hook. Sitting beside a small fire, he grilled it on a stick.

As darkness fell, he sang a prayer song. When he lay down to sleep, the sighing breeze seemed to hold the voices of those who had been here before. Not ghosts, but memories populated his mind.

With his eyes closed, he could see his Oneida mother, Catches the Rainbow, placing fresh split-open fish to be smoked on a rack over the fire. He remembered her smile and her gentle eyes. Her voice was low, and he could not recall her ever raising it in anger—certainly not against him.

His memory of his Oneida father was not so clear. Leaping Deer had been tall, and had had a habit of holding his head slightly turned, as if constantly on the lookout for danger lurking behind his shoulder. For all his wariness, Leaping Deer had died too early, killed in battle at a place called Barren Hill seven moons after he and his wife had adopted Broken Trail.

Broken Trail had learned later that the band's original plan was to hold him for ransom, to trade him for guns and blankets. But Leaping Deer and Catches the Rainbow pleaded to adopt him as a replacement for their own son, who had died. When the band elders approved the adoption, Moses Cobman received the name Broken Trail, and was instructed never to think of himself by his Yengees name again.

As time went by, and especially after Leaping Deer's death, Broken Trail would sometimes waken at night to find Catches the Rainbow, propped on one elbow, watching him with such a look of love that he would close his eyes to shut it out, knowing himself unworthy of so much devotion.

What, he wondered, as he lay under the stars in this place of memories, did Catches the Rainbow think when she thought about him now?

The next day, he travelled on, heading in a southeasterly direction. At dusk, a quick throw of his tomahawk killed a raccoon that was drinking from a stream. A plump, young female. Her meat would be delicious.

After making a small fire and skinning the raccoon, he skewered one haunch on a long stick and settled down to cook his meal. Dripping fat sizzled in the flames, and the mouth-watering smell of roasting meat filled his nostrils.

As he bit into the hot, juicy haunch, a sense of well-being came over him. He liked the way the firelight pushed back the darkness and made the trunks of birch trees gleam white, like a circle of sentinels to guard him.

Suddenly he heard a rustling in the undergrowth, and his whole body jerked to attention. Staring at him were four pairs of round, glowing eyes. Raccoons. A family was watching him eat what might have been their sister. He stopped chewing, ashamed that he had forgotten to apologize to the ghost of the raccoon he had slain.

Before taking another bite, he whispered, "Pardon me. I needed your meat. That is why I had to kill you."

Soon the glowing eyes disappeared. Feeling forgiven, he went back to his meal.

After eating, he wrapped the remaining meat in the raccoon's skin. Then he curled up close to his campfire and fell asleep.

In the morning, voices awoke him—gruff voices conversing in a language that he did not know. He looked out through the slits of his eyelids. Two warriors, both big men, were squatting on the ground, watching him.

One had a turtle tattoo on his bare chest, and the other a snake. Each wore on his belt a polished war club with which he could easily have dashed out Broken Trail's brains. The warriors' heads were shaved except for their scalp locks, which were only a tuft of hair, neatly braided. Oneida warriors did not wear that kind of scalp lock, nor did the warriors of any other Iroquois nation. Who were these men? Leni-Lanape? He hoped so. The Leni-Lanape were friends of his people. But whoever they were, his best defence was to show no fear.

He opened his eyes fully and sat up. The warriors laughed.

Did they laugh because he was just a boy? Or were they laughing at his blue eyes? Blue eyes always made people laugh; but what could he do about it? He must make these warriors understand that he belonged to a nation worthy of respect. Broken Trail tapped his chest.

"Oneida."

They frowned. Maybe they did not understand. He tried again.

"Haudenosaunee."

That worked. Far and wide through the eastern forests, everyone recognized the correct name of the Iroquois, the People of the Longhouse.

"Haudenosaunee?" Both shook their heads. "Yengees." Broken Trail knew that word. "Yengees" meant "English."

He rose to his feet and drew himself up as tall as he could, painfully aware that the top of his head did not reach the chin of either warrior. Maybe if he brandished his tomahawk, they would show respect. But when he pulled it from his belt and waved it threateningly, they laughed again.

What more could he do? An offer of food might show these scoffers that he was a true hunter, a man who knew how to survive in the wilderness. With a sweep of his arm he pointed to the bundled hide that held the rest of the meat.

"Brothers, join me. Here is meat. Let us eat together."

This approach was more successful. They understood his gesture, if not his words. When he had unwrapped the meat, they nodded approvingly.

From embers still alive in the ashes, Broken Trail built up the fire. The warriors cut green sticks from a nearby tree and sharpened the ends to make skewers.

While the meat was cooking, he eyed his visitors curiously. Where were they going? He wanted to tell them that he had been walking for four days and had eight days left in which to reach Kings Mountain. If he knew their language, he could ask how many days' travel lay ahead. But he was no more able to ask than they were to answer.

All three gnawed the meat hungrily. Eating with them made Broken Trail feel like a man among men. When finished, each struck the ground with his right fist while uttering words of thanks to the Great Spirit in his own language.

Then Broken Trail stood up and pointed south to show where his journey lay. When the warriors saw that he meant to leave at once, the one with the snake tattoo took a small rawhide bag from his pouch and handed it to him. Opening it, Broken Trail recognized the honey-coloured powder—finely ground cornmeal mixed with maple sugar. Light to carry and delicious, there was no better food for a long trail. One mouthful, followed by a drink of water, would swell to fill a man's belly. Smiling his thanks, he tucked the bag in his pouch.

For a moment he hoped that the two warriors would travel with him. He had felt grateful for their company after four days without hearing another human voice. But their trail was not his, and he set forth alone.

Chapter 4

BY THE END OF THAT day, his fifth on the trail, he saw in the distance great peaks and ridges jutting into the sky. So he had reached the mountains, and from here on there would be mountains all the way.

"Climbing cuts the distance by half," the captain had told him.

If time had not mattered, Broken Trail would have kept to the valleys, where rivers and streams wound their way. But time did matter. So over the mountains he must go.

He camped overnight in the foothills, and in the morning began to climb. The wooded lower slopes presented no problem. But above the tree line, the ascent was rough and steep. Nothing grew on the high ridges and peaks but lichens and a few stubborn strands of grass.

When he stopped to rest in the late afternoon, he saw a village far below. A Yengees village. Church steeple. Tiny white houses like the one he had lived in long ago. A mill on a creek that twisted and turned and sparkled in the sunshine. There would be fish to catch in a creek like that.

Before they were driven from the Mohawk Valley, Elijah used to take him fishing. They would stand on the riverbank, where the turbulent Canajoharie mixed its waters with the placid Mohawk River, their hooks baited with minnows. Elijah had shown him how to tempt the speckled trout that fed in the swirling water. "That's a beauty!" he would shout as he grabbed his little brother's line to help him land it. Or, "Never mind, there's plenty more where that one came from," when a fish slipped the hook and darted away.

Where was Elijah now? When Broken Trail was nine and his brother thirteen, they had planned to join the Royal Greens together, he as a drummer boy and Elijah as a soldier. If he had not run away, he would be with Elijah now. His name would still be Moses Cobman.

Looking down at the Yengees village, he recalled how different his beginnings had been from those of other Oneida boys. When he went all the way back as far as memory reached, he recalled the feel of a braided rug under his hands and knees, the wide boards of a wood floor, and Ma's hands smelling like bread. His favourite toy had been a red wagon. Never for him a tiny war club or bow and arrows.

It was his duty to forget all this. Why couldn't he?

Broken Trail rose to his feet. He had to keep going if he wanted that rifle. He would climb until sunset, he decided, and then look for a spot of level ground on which to spend the night.

Dark shadows had filled the valley before he found somewhere to sleep—a hard rocky ledge strewn with rubble. It was not a good place, but the best he could find. A massive boulder rested at the edge. Between the boulder and the rock face there was room to lie down. The boulder would stop him from rolling off the ledge in his sleep. Broken Trail shuddered at the thought of his body bouncing and tumbling down the mountainside.

Here there were neither spruce boughs nor piles of fallen leaves to make his bed. No water to drink. And so he could not eat the corn powder in his pouch; instead of giving him a comfortable, well-fed feeling, it would make his stomach ache. With a sigh he took out a hardtack biscuit and began to chew. It tasted no better than last time. His stomach grumbled. He wanted meat. Or a chunk of cornbread. He wanted maple sugar, the sweetness in his throat.

Broken Trail stared at the hardtack that he held between his thumb and finger. Lifting his arm, he hurled it down the mountainside.

Instantly he felt foolish, knowing his action had been childish. Someday he might be grateful for a piece of hardtack, he rebuked himself.

As he watched the sun go down, a bank of dark clouds rolled toward him from the west. The air smelled faintly sulphurous with the approach of thunder, and then the storm broke. Broken Trail crouched between the rock face and the boulder while rain drenched him and thunder cracked so loud it shook the ground.

Even after the storm had passed, he slept little that night. In the morning, he woke up stiff, cold, wet and hungry. Despite the downpour that had pelted him during the storm, he could not find a drop of water to drink. It had all drained away.

Surrounded by rocks and sky, he felt utterly alone. Above him was the crest. Below him vultures circled, probably scouting for some juicy, ripe carcass.

He pulled a hardtack from the bag pouch and this time forced himself to eat it, working hard to produce enough saliva to swallow the dry biscuit. He should have asked those redcoats for a canteen. All he could think about was water, the cool feel of it wetting his mouth, the pleasure of gulping it down. He could hardly wait to reach the next valley. Licking his dry lips, he imagined cool streams and rushing rivers.

On the morning of the eighth day, Broken Trail sat beside a stream, nibbling the sweetened, powdered corn that the two warriors had given him. When he had finished, he knelt and lowered his face to the water.

As he drank, the back of his neck prickled, and he had the feeling that he was being watched. His muscles tensed, and with a single motion he leapt to his feet and pulled his tomahawk from his belt. He saw no one. But suddenly a dry branch snapped.

Broken Trail had his tomahawk ready to hurl when a young warrior stepped, with his right palm raised, from behind a tree. The gesture meant peace, but the youth's face was painted for war, one side black and the other red. He would have looked fierce if the war paint had not been smudged and smeared, as if he had been crawling close to the ground through long grass.

The stranger was taller than Broken Trail, and older. Perhaps fifteen. He wore fringed leather leggings, beaded moccasins and a breechcloth but no shirt. Both sides of his head were shaved, and from his scalp lock dangled three trophy feathers.

He looked exhausted. Maybe he was hungry. Broken Trail held out his bag of corn powder. The stranger's eyes fastened upon it eagerly. Before taking it, he said something in a language that Broken Trail did not recognize, although it sounded a bit like Oneida.

The stranger ate a handful of corn powder and then washed it down with water from the stream. After he had finished, he tapped his chest. "Keetoowah."

"Ah!" This was a word that Broken Trail knew. It meant "Cherokee." The Cherokees were cousins of his people even though they were not part of the Six Nations of the Haudenosaunee. He tapped his own chest. "Oneida."

The response was the usual grunt of disbelief. The Cherokee shook his head and pointed at Broken Trail. "Yengees."

Broken Trail's brow knotted in a savage frown. His blue eyes had betrayed him again.

The Cherokee asked, "You speak English?"

"Yes." Broken Trail hated speaking English, but he was glad that he and this young warrior would be able to talk to each other.

"Why call yourself Oneida? You are white."

Broken Trail was tired of this question, but he answered patiently. "The Oneida adopted me. My name is Broken Trail."

The Cherokee nodded, apparently satisfied with this answer. "I am Red Sun Rising."

"That's a good name."

"What you do in this country, so far from your home?"

"I'm on my way to Kings Mountain."

"Why go there?"

Broken Trail hesitated. Should he tell this stranger about his mission? He knew that the Cherokees hated the white settlers in the mountain valleys. The settlers were treaty breakers, scoffing at treaties that the Cherokees had made in good faith. He decided to take a chance.

"I have a message to deliver to the English commander."

"What sort of message?" Red Sun Rising lay stretched out on the grass, apparently feeling better now that he had something in his stomach.

"A warning that hundreds of Over Mountain men are gathering in a place called Watauga to attack his army. If I'm in time, the redcoats will give me a rifle."

Red Sun Rising gave a low whistle. "A rifle! Do you believe that?"

"The captain who sends the message made that promise. It's in writing. I can read the words."

"In writing . . ." Red Sun Rising looked impressed.

Broken Trail seized the moment. "Come with me. Be my guide."

He half expected the Cherokee to laugh. Red Sun Rising wore three trophy feathers in his scalp lock—three enemies slain in battle. He was a real warrior. Why would he want to go on an adventure with someone like Broken Trail, who still wore his hair long, like a boy?

Red Sun Rising did not laugh. "Yes," he said. "I help you. The English are friends of the Cherokees. They help us defend out land."

"They do?"

"You never hear about Dragging Canoe, our great leader, and his blood brother, Alexander Cameron? Together, they fight the rebels in the Carolinas and Tennessee."

"I reckon there's a lot I don't know."

"You don't know best way through mountains. I show you." Red Sun Rising sat up. He wiped his face with a handful of grass. As he looked at the red and black paint that had come off on the grass, he said, "Two days ago, we make war party against settlers who take our land. They ready for us. They kill everybody but me. Next time I get even. One scalp for every warrior they kill. Five scalps." He held up his hand, fingers splayed. "But first I guide you to Kings Mountain. That is a long trail. Six days."

"I need to get there in four. The captain told me I had twelve days to reach Kings Mountain. This is the eighth."

Red Sun Rising stood up, his fatigue apparently forgotten. "We start now."

Chapter 5

RED SUN RISING LED Broken Trail through a narrow mountain pass that he never could have found on his own. As he scrambled and climbed after his guide, he felt a growing sense of confidence now that Red Sun Rising was in charge, even though the Cherokee gave no assurances that they would reach Kings Mountain in time.

As daylight faded, they stopped beside a rushing stream where water tumbled over the rocks, cascading from pool to pool. A few low bushes grew here, but no trees. Broken Trail pulled his little bag of sweetened corn powder from his pouch and passed it to Red Sun Rising. After they had eaten and drunk, Red Sun Rising scooped up a handful of coarse sand from the bottom of the stream and with it scrubbed his face, removing every trace of the smeared war paint.

"We rest here tonight," he said. "In morning we go on."

"Do you think we can reach Kings Mountain in three days?"

"We try."

Drawing little encouragement from this answer, Broken Trail felt his hope for a rifle begin to fade. He would have pushed on without sleeping if Red Sun Rising had suggested it, despite the obvious peril of traversing mountain passes in the dark.

Red Sun Rising interrupted his thoughts.

"When you get that rifle," he said, his voice full of energy, as if he had never entertained the slightest doubt, "you come with me to Chickamauga. That is my town. I tell my friends, Broken Trail looks white, but his heart is same like ours. You join our war party. We kill settlers. Take many scalps."

Broken Trail hated to refuse Red Sun Rising, who was going to so much trouble to help him on his mission. He even liked the idea of joining a war party, but it was more important to return home as soon as he could. Besides, he was not sure that he wanted to kill settlers.

"Is every settler an enemy?" he asked hesitantly.

"Every one is our enemy. Every settler steals Cherokee land. Our chiefs make treaties. They give up much land. Settlers promise to take no more. They break that promise.

Our chiefs make a new treaty. They give more land. Settlers break promise again. Every time, they push us farther into lands of other nations. The Koasati and the Muskogees don't want us there. It's their land. Then our leader Dragging Canoe tells us, 'Kill all the settlers before they push us into the Mississippi River.'"

"You can't trust white people," Broken Trail agreed. "We Oneidas helped the rebels. But General Sullivan burned our towns anyway. Burned our fields. Left us hungry with nowhere to live."

"Kill them all!"

With these words, Red Sun Rising lay down, rolled onto his side, and rested his head upon his folded arm. "Time to sleep," he said in a voice so fierce that Broken Trail wondered what kind of dreams he was likely to have.

Lying down near him, Broken Trail closed his eyes. Though the stony ground was no more comfortable than the mountain ledge on which he had slept three nights ago, he dozed off quickly. And then he dreamed.

In his dream he was back in the forest glade of his spirit quest. As before, the wolverine walked out of the bushes and stood looking at him. It was just as big and shaggy and its teeth were just as sharp and yellow as when he had seen it in his trance. And the musky smell was just as strong. But this time the wolverine said nothing. After staring at Broken Trail for a few moments, it raised its head and walked away. As it disappeared into the undergrowth, it glanced back over its shoulder, as if inviting Broken Trail to follow.

He wanted to follow. But when he tried to rise, he could not move. He wanted to call out to the wolverine, but could make no sound. Suddenly he awoke. Opening his eyes, he saw Red Sun Rising lying fast asleep, but no wolverine was anywhere about. Gone again, he thought. Then he sniffed the air and smiled. Wolverine. There was no mistaking that pungent smell.

Settling down to sleep again, he let his mind linger over the recollection of his dream, hoping to slide back into it. But that one brief vision was all that the spirits allowed.

After one more day in the mountains, Red Sun Rising and Broken Trail descended into a valley, following a clear, wide track between wooded slopes. Broken Trail saw horses' hoof prints in the soft earth.

"Soon we come to settlers' farms," Red Sun Rising said. "Over Mountain men."

So far, Broken Trail had seen no sign of settlement, for there was nothing but forest on either side of the track. He was beginning to wonder where the settlers and their farms might be, when he and Red Sun Rising rounded a bend and he saw, down a short lane, a log cabin surrounded by tree stumps.

In the spaces between the stumps were the withered stems and the brown leaves of turnip and potato plants, as well as freshly turned soil where these root vegetables had been dug. But he saw no sign of a human being, a horse, a cow, a pig, or any other living creature. Everything was quiet. The cabin door stood ajar. No smoke rose from the chimney. The sight gave Broken Trail a shivery feeling. Something was amiss.

"Nobody there," he said.

"We look."

They crept forward cautiously. Broken Trail clutched his tomahawk. Red Sun Rising had his knife ready. When they peered around the edge of the half-open door, Broken Trail smelled the acrid odour of a burnt-out fire mingled with the sweet, stale smell of blood.

From the doorway he saw a long plank table in the middle of the room. On the table sat the remnants of a meal. Flies clustered about ham slices on a platter. There were broken biscuits on tin plates.

Half under the table, clinging to each other, were the bodies of two little girls in matching homespun gowns. They appeared to be five or six years old. Twins, perhaps. Beside one table leg lay a cloth doll with tufts of yellow yarn for hair, and a happy smile embroidered on its face.

Broken Trail stepped into the room. Now he saw the rest.

Near one wall, a man wearing a grey hemp shirt and black breeches lay crumpled beside an overturned chair. Broken Trail flinched when he saw the bloody top of his head where his scalp had been.

Sprawled upon the hearth was the body of a young woman. She lay on her back, her face nearly as white as her apron. The blood in which she lay had dried almost black. A dead baby lay beside its cradle on the plank floor.

Every scalp had been sliced off. Blood was splattered everywhere.

"We're too late." Red Sun Rising returned his knife to his belt.

Broken Trail could not take his eyes from the baby. It was so small. He wanted to pick up the baby and return it to its cradle. But he couldn't do that with Red Sun Rising watching, his dark eyes hard as stone.

"Come on. Let's go," Broken Trail took a step backward, pulling his foot free from the stickiness on the floor.

"Not yet. Maybe we find guns."

Red Sun Rising went into the next room, leaving Broken Trail staring at the baby.

When he returned, he was holding a straight razor. "No guns. Nothing good but this, Very sharp."

"It's for shaving."

Red Sun Rising's face creased in a grim smile. "When you get that rifle, I use this to shave your head, except for scalp lock. We put on war paint. We find plenty more settlers." He waved his arm in a gesture that seemed to dismiss the five bodies. "Take many scalps."

Broken Trail turned his face away. He crossed to the threshold and stood gazing out at the tree stumps and empty yard, for he could not bear to look any longer at the massacred family.

"Hurry," he said. "Let's not waste more time."

He walked out through the open doorway without looking back.

Those settlers had no right to steal Cherokee land. But it wasn't right, either, to kill helpless people while they were eating supper in their own home.

Whose side was he on, he wondered, when both sides were in the wrong? He wanted to help Red Sun Rising, but he did not want to be part of his war. Killing settlers was not the answer. There had to be a better way.

Chapter 6

THE SUN HAD STOOD straight overhead when Broken Trail and Red Sun Rising left the cabin of the murdered family. They had been walking ever since. Now the sun was setting, yet they had not once paused to eat or to rest.

"When will we stop for the night?" Broken Trail asked.

"Not stop. Not this night. Not next night. Then maybe we come to Kings Mountain in time."

Maybe? Broken Trail thought this over. *Maybe* was not reassuring. He was already tired. How could they walk two nights and two days without a rest? Not even the toughest warrior could manage that. And even if they could, they still might be too late.

Broken Trail's heart sank. He had been travelling for ten days, and if he did not reach Kings Mountain in time, it would be all for naught.

Despite his discouraging words, Red Sun Rising showed no sign of wanting to give up. Fatigue did not slow him. If anything, he walked faster.

Before it grew dark, they passed half a dozen more homesteads, each in its own clearing, and once they made a wide circle through the woods in order to avoid a village. The name of the village was Elizabethtown, Red Sun Rising told him, and it was not safe for them to be seen there.

A full moon hung in the black sky when Red Sun Rising suddenly stopped walking. He pointed to a homestead nestled in a hollow just off the track. Visible in the moonlight were a two-storey house of dressed timbers, a small barn and a smaller outbuilding. The windows of the house were dark. In a paddock, standing nose to tail with their heads lowered in sleep, stood two horses. One was dark, the other light in colour, though it was too dark to tell what that colour might be.

"Horses," said Red Sun Rising. "We take them. Ride all night."

Ride all night! Everybody knew that Cherokee boys could ride before they could walk. But Broken Trail had never been on a horse. He did not like this idea. But what excuse could he give, apart from admitting that he might fall off?

"I'm not sure we ought to do that. People hang horse thieves."

"Only if they catch them."

"What if there's a dog? It'll wake up everybody."

"I have spell to make dog quiet." As if he sensed Broken Trail's reluctance, he added quickly, "These are the horses of our enemies. It is right to take them." When Broken Trail continued to hesitate, Red Sun Rising said bluntly, "Don't you want to reach Kings Mountain in two days?"

Broken Trail gulped. "I can't . . . I can't . . ."

"You can't ride!" The Cherokee's voice mixed amusement with disbelief. "I teach you fast."

Reaching into his pouch, he pulled out two pieces of cord and made a loop at one end of each. "Cord go in horse's mouth. Like this." Without warning, he grabbed Broken Trail's jaw, pulled it open, and looped his lower jaw.

"Ow!" Startled rather than hurt, Broken Trail pulled the cord off.

Red Sun Rising took it from him. "I put it on horse for you. You pull cord. Tell your horse which way to go."

Broken Trail understood. During his childhood in Canajoharie he had been familiar with bits and halters although his family had not owned a horse.

The boys crept like lynxes through the underbrush. When they neared the house, Red Sun Rising gave a whistle. He waited, and then whistled a second time. Sure enough, a shaggy black and white dog emerged from the shadows beside the front step. The dog shook itself and then turned its head this way and that, its ears pricked up.

Red Sun Rising raised his arm. Something flew through

the air. The dog sniffed, picked it up, and carried it away.

Now the horses were awake. Their ears angled forward. Broken Trail heard their snorting breath.

"Which one you want?" Red Sun Rising whispered.

"I don't care."

"Then I take the dark horse."

Red Sun Rising inched forward and eased open the paddock gate. First, he stroked the light horse's neck, and then he deftly slipped the loop of the cord around its lower jaw. The horse did not object. Then he did the same to the dark horse.

"Ready?" he whispered. Without a sound, he sprang onto the back of the dark horse. It stamped its feet and whinnied.

"Hurry," he whispered to Broken Trail, who crouched close to the paddock fence, hoping that his *oki* was near. Tightening his muscles, he leapt. If he had not grabbed a handful of mane, he might have shot over the horse and landed on the other side. But in a moment he had thrown one leg over the horse's back and gained his balance.

Red Sun Rising grabbed the free end of the cord that dangled from the jaw of Broken Trail's horse. He handed the cord to Broken Trail before reaching across to slap the pale horse's rump. Both horses shot out of the paddock and up the lane to the track, with the dark horse in the lead.

Broken Trail lay forward against his horse's warm neck, one fist clutching the mane, and the other the end of the cord. He gripped with his legs as hard as he could while the horse rocked him up and down and back and forth all at the same time. He slid sideways. He was going to fall off. *"Oki! Oki!"* He whimpered. "Save me!" Behind him he heard shouts and rifle fire.

There was no pursuit. How could there have been, with the horses gone? After a brief gallop, Red Sun Rising slowed his horse to a canter, and then a trot. Broken Trail, pulling cautiously on the cord, was surprised at the willingness of his horse to obey. They kept going for the rest of the night.

At sunrise Red Sun Rising stopped his horse and slid from its back. He held out one hand to help Broken Trail dismount.

"The Oneida are great warriors," he stated, "but not great horsemen."

Broken Trail's thighs hurt and his knees wobbled. "I praise the Earth, my mother," he said weakly. Good solid unmoving Mother Earth.

They led the horses from the track into the forest. When he had caught his breath, Broken Trail said, "The dog didn't bark. What spell did you use?"

"Dried blood and bear grease stuffed into a hollow bone. Powerful magic, but it only works on dogs. I carry it on war party, but settlers see us before I can use it." Red Sun Rising gave a shake of his head as if to banish an unwelcome thought. "Let us hobble these horses. They need to rest. So do we. No one can catch us before we reach Kings Mountain. We are there in two days. You give your message in time."

Chapter 7

RED SUN RISING pointed through the streaming rain toward a flat-topped hill a mile away.

"Kings Mountain," he said.

"That's no mountain!"

"Yengees give it that name, not me."

The steep sides of the hill looked as if they ought to continue up and up into the sky. The Maker of All Things had a mountain in mind, Broken Trail thought, when he planted the base. But sixty feet above the surrounding plain, the mountain stopped. It looked as if a giant had sliced off the rest and carried it away, leaving only a bare, flat top.

Broken Trail took a deep breath and then exhaled slowly.

He had reached his destination in twelve days. He would deliver his message on time.

His legs gripped the horse's sides as it jounced along the trail, and he muttered a prayer of thanks to his *oki* for keeping him safe so far. Even little problems, like steering the horse, had become manageable. Now all he had to do was deliver the message and collect his new rifle. A sentry could direct him to Major Ferguson's tent, the English captain had said.

The rain had lessened by the time he and Red Sun Rising reached the foot of Kings Mountain. They stopped by a small stream, dismounted and hobbled their horses, leaving them to graze amongst the trees—great oaks and maples draped in moss.

"Horses not go far," Red Sun Rising said. "We ride away soon."

The sides of Kings Mountain were heavily wooded with mature trees big enough for a man to hide behind. They climbed the steep slope.

At the top, Broken Trail and Red Sun Rising emerged onto the bald plateau, which was twice as long as it was wide. One end was open field; the other was covered with army tents. Apart from a few soldiers piling heaps of rocks near the edge of the plateau, Broken Trail saw no sign of defence preparations.

"This army doesn't look ready for battle," he said. "They must think nobody can get at them from below."

Red Sun Rising looked down at the thick cover of trees on the steep incline.

"Then they make big mistake."

"I don't see a sentry. Maybe we should ask those soldiers piling rocks for directions to Major Ferguson's tent."

"Don't need to ask. I see it."

He pointed along a line of identical army tents to one that was twice the size of the rest. It had a sheet of canvas stretched horizontally over the opening as an awning. Under the canvas, protected from the drizzle, stood two soldiers leaning on their muskets, looking half asleep.

"Yes. That must be it," Broken Trail said.

When the soldiers noticed the boys approaching, both stood a little straighter and pointed their muskets in a half-hearted way. Broken Trail raised his right hand, open palm outward, in the sign of peace.

"I bring a message for Major Patrick Ferguson."

Those words seemed to wake them up. The corners of their eyes crinkled with amusement as they looked the boys over. As usual, Broken Trail's blue eyes claimed chief attention.

One of the soldiers smiled, showing broken teeth. "What are *you* doing, dressed up like an Indian?"

Broken Trail summoned all the dignity he could muster. "What I look like doesn't matter. I bring a message for Major Ferguson. I've been travelling twelve days to deliver it to him and to nobody else."

The other soldier, who had a snub nose and freckles, snorted. "The boy's a half-breed. They sometimes come out looking pretty white."

"Those can be the worst kind of devils," the soldier with broken teeth said.

Broken Trail scowled. "Look at this!" He pulled the letter from his pouch. "Take me to Major Ferguson."

"Oh, we dassn't do that," he snickered. "A brave like you might lift his scalp, and then where would we be?"

"What's the message?" said the other soldier, smirking. "We can let him know as soon as he's disposed. At the moment, the Major is entertaining a lady."

"Is that what you'd call Virginia Sal?" his comrade snickered.

Both burst out laughing. Broken Trail gave them a dark look as he shoved the letter under their very noses.

"Read the cover."

"I can't read," said the soldier with broken teeth.

"No more can I," the other grinned.

"The message is addressed to Major Patrick Ferguson, and it's marked 'Urgent.'"

"Who taught *you* to read!"

The soldier with broken teeth spat on the ground. "Maybe we should tell Captain DePeyster. Keep ourselves in the clear if there be something to it."

"Nobody could attack us here."

"That's God's truth. But I'm going to tell DePeyster all

the same." He turned to the boys. "Wait here. I'll to talk to Major Ferguson's aide." Leaving the shelter of the awning, he strode to the tent just beyond.

Inside the major's tent, Broken Trail heard a woman speak, then a man. After a moment, the woman began to sing. Her voice was clear and sweet. Broken Trail strained to hear the words:

It was in and about the Martinmas time,
When the green leaves were a falling,
That Sir John Graeme in the West Country
Fell in love with Barbara Allan.

Had he heard this song before? The words? The melody? Had Ma sung it to him many years ago? The song was so pretty that it made him shiver.

He sent his man down through the town,
To the place where she was dwelling:
"O haste and come to my master dear,
Gin ye be Barbara Allan."

Before he could hear more, the soldier returned, stepping along briskly at the side of an officer in full dress uniform, including a sword, a white wig and a tricorn hat. The officer thrust out his hand.

"Let's see this message."

"No. It's for Major Ferguson's eyes alone."

"I'm his aide. It has to go through me."

Broken Trail tightened his grip on the letter.

"Come, boy, give it over. If you waste more of my time, I'll have you whipped."

Broken Trail considered charging in upon Major Ferguson and his companion. Then Ferguson would be forced to pay attention. It was worth a try.

Taking a quick sideways step, he bolted under DePeyster's arm, and rushed the tent. Not quick enough. The freckle-faced soldier grabbed his shoulder and spun him about. The other soldier's big hand seized Broken Trail's wrist, wrested the message from him and passed it to the officer.

"Here you are, sir."

DePeyster squinted at the cover. "Urgent, eh?" He read the back. "If this reaches you, give the bearer a rifle for his trouble."

He snorted, "Oh no, my lad, a trick like this won't work," and tossed the letter away. It landed in a puddle. "What scallywag wrote that for you?"

Without waiting for an answer, he said to the soldiers, "The message is a forgery. But you did well to be vigilant. We're only twenty-five miles west of Charlotte. Lord Cornwallis will be here in a day or two with the main army to relieve us. As for these rascals . . .," he turned to the soldier with broken teeth, "Corporal, you can escort them quick march out of camp."

"Yes, sir."

"But the captain promised—" Broken Trail could hardly speak for anger.

"Get moving!" DePeyster barked.

Red Sun Rising gave Broken Trail a warning glance from the corner of his eye. "I think we leave this place." With chin up, he started walking. Broken Trail squared his shoulders and followed, doing his best to preserve what dignity he could.

The words of the woman's song followed him:

O mother, mother, make my bed!
O make it soft and narrow!
Since my love died for me today
I'll die for him tomorrow.

The sadness of the words touched Broken Trail's heart, softening his anger. Like the lady in the song, he had suffered a loss. For him, too, something had died. A dream.

At the edge of the plateau, the soldiers were still piling rocks. One of them happened to be facing him, and Broken Trail saw on his forage cap the green badge of the King's Own Regiment. The soldier was bending over to lay a rock upon the pile. Then he straightened and raised his face.

When he saw that face, Broken Trail felt as if a lightning bolt had struck. The blue eyes that met his were his brother's eyes. He could not utter a sound.

"Moses?" Elijah took one step forward. He stared at Broken Trail with a mixture of shock and disbelief.

"Back to work, private!" someone shouted. Elijah did not move.

Between his shoulders Broken Trail felt a jab. "Keep going!"

The next jab was harder, making him stumble forward. The soldier laughed and gave him another jab. From the harshness of his laughter, Broken Trail suspected that he would welcome any excuse to shoot.

They reached the edge of the plateau.

"Away with you," the soldier snarled. "Don't show your ugly faces around here ever again!" He turned on his heels and left.

It had stopped raining.

Broken Trail moved in a daze as he started down the hill. The captain's message lying in the mud was forgotten. The rifle was forgotten. His brother's face was the only image stamped on his mind.

Chapter 8

IF BROKEN TRAIL DID not trip over roots or bump into trees as he descended the hill, it was only because, in a mechanical, automatic way, his senses still worked. Yet he was not really aware of his surroundings until suddenly Red Sun Rising grabbed his arm and hauled him behind a large oak tree.

"What is it?" Broken Trail asked, jolted alert.

"Shh!" Red Sun Rising laid a finger on Broken Trail's lips. With a turn of his head, he motioned down the hill. "Look there!"

A flash of white. Something moved. It looked like a man wearing a white gown nearly to his knees.

"That's an Over Mountain man," Red Sun Rising whispered.

"Dressed like a woman?"

"It's what they wear."

"No uniforms?"

"They put on long shirts over their other clothes."

Peering from behind the tree, Broken Trail saw, near the bottom of the hill, another white-shirted man, and then another, and another. The hillside swarmed with Over Mountain men advancing up the hill toward them. And that was not all. Mingled with them were just as many soldiers in blue uniforms.

"They not see us yet," murmured Red Sun Rising.

"But they will. In a minute they'll be all around us. We can't stay behind this tree."

Red Sun Rising pointed to a dense clump of low-growing junipers. "Hide in there. Hurry!"

Broken Trail pulled away. "No! I must go back. Warn the soldiers."

"You crazy? They not listen to you. Too late anyway."

Broken Trail hesitated. For his brother he would risk his life. But there was no way that he could reach the top of Kings Mountain without the rebels seeing him. And even if he reached the top and made the redcoats heed his warning, it would be too late.

He dropped to the ground and, on all fours, crawled after Red Sun Rising into the juniper clump. Here, as long as they lay still, the low-arching branches with their thick needles would conceal them. Their deerskin clothing was almost the same colour as the fallen needles that covered the ground—a perfect camouflage.

They lay flat on their stomachs, the juniper's twisted trunk between their bodies and their heads so close together that Broken Trail could hear Red Sun Rising's quick breathing. Through the juniper's drooping branches, Broken Trail saw little of what was happening, but he could hear everything.

Silently the enemy climbed. The first rank passed the juniper clump. Broken Trail watched feet go by. Feet in army boots. Feet in moccasins. Wave after wave, from tree to tree, the rebel force moved up the hill.

With a sinking heart, Broken Trail thought of Elijah up there on top of Kings Mountain. In his mind's eye he saw him still piling rocks, heedless and unaware, setting one stone on top of another in that futile, half-hearted effort to build a barricade.

The rebels' advance halted. Through the juniper's branches Broken Trail saw a pair of sturdy legs in army boots little more than an arm's length from his nose.

He heard the thumping of his own heart, but no other sound. The waiting army held its breath. Not one whisper, not one cough broke the silence. The woods felt hushed.

The first crack of rifle fire came from the south side of Kings Mountain, a hundred yards away. Then noise exploded all around.

"Charge!" The shout was so close that Broken Trail jumped. "On them! Over the top!"

Up the hill the rebels swept.

So close to the plateau's edge, Elijah would be one of the first to face the charge. Unarmed. Or would he have time to grab his rifle? Broken Trail thought he heard his brother's voice in the shouting from the top. It could have been anyone.

"Fire!" came the command from above. Bullets clattered among the trees. The Loyal Americans were shooting back. Elijah, too? A piercing whistle blew. Men shouted. Horses whinnied. The whistle shrilled from a different quarter, then from somewhere else. That was the last time.

From above came a final hail of bullets. The shooting stopped.

Was it over? The battle had lasted no longer than it would take a hunter to skin a deer.

Broken Trail pressed his cheek against the carpet of juniper needles and fought back tears. He tried not to picture Elijah lying dead. Surely the Great Spirit would not have granted one brief glimpse of his brother, only to snatch him away again! It would be so unfair. But was life ever fair?

"Give no quarter!" came a shout. "Remember Waxhaws!"

Atop Kings Mountain, someone shouted, "Search the slopes! Use your bayonets! Don't let anyone get away!"

Broken Trail tore his thoughts away from Elijah. "We can't stay here," he whispered to Red Sun Rising.

"Safer to stay. Maybe they not see us."

"But if they do, we're dead. I'm leaving. I'd rather be shot running than stuck with a bayonet lying down."

"Wait. We need a signal. You want help, you call me. I want help, I call you."

"What kind of signal?"

"Saw-whet owl. Like this." He whistled a mellow note: "*Too, too, too, too.*"

Broken Trail imitated the sound.

"Good. Don't forget."

Wriggling from under the juniper boughs, Broken Trail dashed to the nearest tree. Safe for the moment behind its trunk, he looked down the side of Kings Mountain. Where could he find a hiding place to crawl into until the men with bayonets had finished their search? A cave? A crevice?

At the bottom of the hill stood a huge maple, its heavy branches draped with moss. Dense brush hid the bottom of its trunk. He had seen other trees like that in the southern valleys, some with roots half exposed above the floodplain and a washout cavity underneath. He skidded down the slope over leaves slick with rain and dived into the tangle of green growth. Yes! There was a hole, and it was big enough. After crawling in, he reached outside to pull a curtain of vines across the opening.

If anyone tracked him here, he was doomed. But to detect this hole, a man would have to lie on his belly and pull the vines aside.

Broken Trail breathed a quick prayer to the Great Spirit,

not just for his own safety but also for the safety of his brother and of his friend. As his eyes adjusted to the dim light, he saw the tree's dark inner bark and a mass of spider webs. The cavity was large enough to be a hiding place for two people, although they would be cramped.

Beginning to relax, he inhaled a deep breath of clammy air. Under the rank, sour smell of decaying vegetation, he caught the scent of wolverine. He sniffed again. That unique, musky smell. Nothing else stank like that. His *oki* had not left him.

Chapter 9

MEN WERE COMING DOWN the hill, their feet crashing through the undergrowth. Crouching inside the cavity under the maple tree, Broken Trail held his breath.

"Use your bayonets," someone shouted. "Don't let any of those redcoats get away."

Broken Trail heard a scream. More shouts. More crashing about. Another command. The shouting and crashing went on and on. Tense and sweating, he prayed for it to end soon.

Finally a voice called out, "Back to the top. Looks like we're finished here." A harsh laugh. "We've more to do up there before dark."

The voices grew more distant, until the call of a mockingbird was the loudest distinct sound he could hear.

Broken Trail breathed more easily, and with every breath inhaled the lingering scent of wolverine. He felt safe knowing that his *oki* was watching over him. Without its help, he never could have found this hiding place.

Settling down to rest, he felt under his body something crumbly, like sawdust. It was soft, and neither wet nor dry. He would not like to be trapped in a washout cavity during a spring flood; but in early fall when water levels were low, the space was comfortable enough.

When he turned his head, he saw a slender beam of light that wavered in the darkness, piercing the leafy vines that concealed the opening of the cavity. His eyes fastened upon the light. Now and then, fluttering leaves blocked the little beam, but each time it reappeared in a moment. He reached out his hand so that it fell upon his skin, a quivering spot of light no larger than the nail of his little finger.

It was a sign, he thought. The unseen spirits often communicated in such a way, using something as natural as a ray of sunshine, a rainbow or a falling star to send a message. Looking at the trembling spot of light, he felt sure that it had been sent to give him hope. His mission had failed. The soldiers had laughed at him. His brother was probably dead. Yet at a time when all his effort seemed a complete waste, this tiny light had appeared in the darkness. It was not enough to make clear the pathways of his life, but it was enough to give assurance that something was guiding his footsteps. He had been right to feel, on setting forth, that this mission belonged to him, just as his *oki* belonged to him. The Great Spirit, he saw now for the first time, had a plan for his life.

When the sun set and the little light vanished for the last time, Broken Trail closed his eyes. In the morning he would try to learn the fate of his brother and of his friend. Although his mind seethed with questions, his exhausted body demanded sleep. The last sound he heard was a cricket chirping almost in his ear.

That night the spirits sent a dark dream in which he saw Elijah, wearing his tricorn hat with its green badge, lying wounded on the battlefield among the bloodied corpses of many men and horses. Broken Trail tried to run to him, but it was as if his ankles were hobbled together and he seemed to be running in one spot, running and running, but still no closer. His throat ached with the vain effort to shout that he was on his way. Harder and harder he ran, knowing that Elijah would die if he could not reach him soon. Then, unexpectedly, Elijah rose up and stood with one arm raised, the palm of his hand turned forward in salute. Broken Trail saw that what had been a tricorn hat with a green badge had become a scalp lock from which three trophy feathers trailed. The face he saw was no longer Elijah's but Red Sun Rising's, painted red and black for war.

Broken Trail woke abruptly from his nightmare. To him

its meaning was clear enough. His brother needed him. Red Sun Rising needed him. He felt helpless, not knowing what he could do, and did not fall asleep again until it was nearly dawn.

Voices roused him. The voices were very close, right outside his hiding place. Through the vines he saw daylight. He lay still, listening.

"Well, Jed, we surely did a fine job yesterday." The voice had a nasal twang.

"So we did." This speaker had a deeper voice. "Every damn redcoat either dead or taken prisoner. We got 'em all."

"Not all. There's plenty more where this lot came from."

"What d'you mean, George? Did y'all see something suspicious?"

"Jed, it ain't what I already seen, it's what I know is coming. General Cornwallis, I mean to say. He'll likely get here tomorrow with the main army. When he does, I sure as hell don't plan to be around. I'm going home."

"I'll travel with y'all," Jed answered. "I figure my proper place is back in the Watauga Valley protecting my wife and young'uns from those damn Cherokees. Besides, I got a nice present to give my boy."

"What's that?"

"Silver whistle."

"Why, you lucky son-of-a-gun! Ferguson's silver whistle! I'll give you five pounds for that."

"Not for sale."

"Did you see who got his hunting shirt?"

"Who'd want it with eight bullet holes?"

"I would," George answered. "I'd cherish every one."

"Ferguson was a goddamn fool, riding around with that checkered shirt over his uniform. Just daring us to shoot him."

"Well, we certainly obliged." George laughed. "Right out of the saddle!"

"Benjamin Cleveland got his horse."

"Cleveland! Pity the poor horse! Cleveland weighs close to three hundred pounds. You could make two Pat Fergusons out of a man that size."

Both chuckling, the two men walked on.

Broken Trail stayed quiet and still a little longer, wanting to be certain that no more Over Mountain men were nearby. As soon as it seemed safe, he pushed aside the vines and crawled out of the hole.

His heart filled with hope and dread as he climbed the steep slope. Silently he approached the juniper clump and pulled apart the low, spreading branches. Nothing. Not so much as a drop of blood to stain the scuffed needles. He felt limp with relief. "*Too, too, too,*" he whistled. No response. He had not really expected one. Maybe he would find Red Sun Rising at the top of Kings Mountain, on the battlefield. Maybe he would find Elijah, too.

Chapter 10

BROKEN TRAIL PASSED the unfinished barricade, where a dead soldier lay slumped over a pile of rocks. He was not Elijah.

Now Broken Trail saw before him a shambles of freshly dug graves, dead horses and dead men. Every human corpse wore a scarlet tunic. Not worth the rebels' trouble to bury redcoats, he reckoned. He wondered about Major Ferguson and Virginia Sal, but saw no trace of a dead man in a checkered hunting shirt or of a woman.

The tent where Virginia Sal had sung her ballad stood tilted but intact, one end of its awning hanging loose and its flap open. Looking inside, Broken Trail saw a polished wooden box with brass corners lying upon a woven carpet beside a smashed camp table.

Major Ferguson's quarters had fared better than most. Where one day ago trim white tents had stood, Broken Trail now saw sagging canvas draped over leaning poles.

The vultures were arriving. Some had landed; more circled on V-spread wings. A few steps to one side, a vulture swooped down to land on the chest of a drummer boy. Broken Trail pulled out his tomahawk. Before he could hurl it, the vulture lifted into the air and settled a moment later upon a different corpse.

Broken Trail stood thoughtfully at the side of the drummer boy. He was a small boy with blond curls, not more than ten years old. Broken Trail picked up his drum and tapped it with his fingertips. A drummer boy was what he had wanted to be when he was nine. If he and Elijah had enlisted together the way they had planned, that might have been him, lying cold and stiff and still. Where was Elijah now? Broken Trail set down the drum and continued walking, searching for the body that he did not want to find.

A sudden shout disturbed the silence.

"Ho! Broken Trail!"

There was Red Sun Rising, striding toward him. He was wearing an officer's scarlet coat, ornamented in front with gold lace on a dark blue velvet ground. An epaulette of gold fringe hung from each shoulder.

At the sight of Red Sun Rising alive, Broken Trail felt as

if the sun had broken through heavy clouds. "You escaped!" he shouted.

"I told you that was good place to hide." Red Sun Rising ran the last few steps and whacked Broken Trail on the back. "How you like my new coat?" He grinned as he turned around to show the back. "No bullet holes."

The coat was bloody around the stand-up collar, but otherwise unmarked.

"It's good." Broken Trail felt like laughing, partly from relief and partly from amusement at the sight of scuffed deerskin leggings below the splendid scarlet coat.

"Now we leave this place," said Red Sun Rising. "Find horses."

"Not yet." Broken Trail glanced around the battlefield. "I'm looking for something."

"No guns here. Soldiers and Over Mountain men take every one."

"I'm looking for . . . a hat." Broken Trail felt suddenly defensive. He could not explain about Elijah. Not here. Not now. Red Sun Rising, walking ahead, had not seen the young soldier who left off piling rocks to step forward and call out, "Moses." And even if Red Sun Rising had heard it, the name would have meant nothing to him.

"Hat no good. Why not get new coat?" With a shake of his shoulders, he set the golden fringes of the epaulettes swinging. "Be quick. I wait where we leave horses."

"Just a minute. Tell me. Did the rebels take prisoners?"

"Many, many prisoners. Like trees in the forest."

"Where did they go with them?"

"I don't know."

"Well, what direction?"

Red Sun Rising pointed north. "That way."

"When?"

"At sunrise."

"Only this morning?"

Red Sun Rising nodded. "Everybody make camp here all night. They leave this morning."

"Then they can't have gone far." Broken Trail looked northward, as if he still might see the army marching away. All he saw was a rutted, muddy track winding into the distance before it disappeared between wooded hills.

"Now I look for horses," Red Sun Rising said. "I wait for you."

"No. Don't wait. If you find the horses . . ." He hesitated. "If the horses are still there, take one and leave without me."

"But you travel with me to Chickamauga."

Broken Trail shook his head. "I must go home."

"You not come with me?" He sighed. "I think all times maybe you not come."

Broken Trail turned his face away. He wished that he knew how to repay his friend for having guided him all the way to Kings Mountain. But making war on white settlers was not the right way. Besides, it was certainly true that he must go home.

"Someday we'll meet again," Broken Trail said, not believing that they ever would. He forced himself to meet the Cherokee's gaze as they clasped hands in farewell. "Be strong," he added, for that was the Oneida way to say goodbye.

His eyes followed Red Sun Rising, resplendent in the scarlet coat with its shining adornments, until he was out of sight down the hill. Then Broken Trail renewed his search.

It was very quiet. Hard to imagine that only yesterday screams, gunfire and the shrill blast of a silver whistle had rent the air. Broken Trail walked on and on, crossing the battlefield back and forth.

As he walked, he wondered what Carries a Quiver would think if he could see him now. Many times his uncle had instructed him to forget his white family. Always, Broken Trail had hidden the fact that he could not. For a long time he had felt ashamed about his feelings as well as about deceiving his uncle. He still felt guilty about the deception, but somewhere along the way to Kings Mountain his opinion had changed about the rest. To care about Elijah was not wrong, nor did not make him any less an Oneida. Or did it?

Broken Trail was mulling over this question when right at his feet he saw, lying in the mud, a forage cap displaying a green badge.

Just a cap. No fallen soldier nearby. He picked up the cap. It was a cocked hat made of coarse felt, bound with white tape. Inside the band, he found a long, brown hair. That proved nothing. Elijah had brown hair. So did he. So did half the white people he had ever known.

Broken Trail pulled his knife from its sheath, severed the threads that attached the badge to the cap, and thrust the badge into his pouch. Maybe it wasn't Elijah's. But maybe it was.

He walked across to the north side of the plateau and, looking down, studied the deep ruts from wagon wheels and the prints of horses' hooves and men's boots. With wounded to tend and prisoners to guard, the army could not be making rapid progress. He should be able to catch up in half a day. Then he would shadow the army, skulking in the bushes to scan the prisoners' faces. If Elijah was there, he would rescue him. Somehow, he would find a way.

Chapter 11

HE HEARD THE ARMY before he saw it. First the creaking and rumbling of heavy wagons reached his ears, then the voices of men: officers barking orders, soldiers talking and the wounded crying out. He walked faster, and as soon as he rounded the next bend, the wagons were in sight, bringing up the rear of the army.

Now he slipped into the cover of the trees along the track. Like a wolf shadowing a herd of deer, he moved silently through the woods.

He watched the heavy draught horses labour to pull the wagons. No wonder he had caught up so quickly! The wagon wheels were over their rims in mud.

From a distance, he had thought that the wagons were loaded with supplies. When he drew nearer, he saw that what they carried were wounded men—soldiers in blue uniforms, lying or sitting on the floorboards. No redcoats were among them.

Ahead of the wagons, the prisoners walked three or four abreast in a disorderly column. Their red tunics, which had been bright and clean one day before, were soiled with mud and blood. Flanking the prisoners, two on each side, were the rebel soldiers guarding them. Fixed to the guards' muskets were bayonets, with which they jabbed the prisoners from time to time to keep them moving.

Many of the prisoners looked barely able to walk. They shuffled along, some so weak they stumbled with every step. The healthier-looking prisoners were laden like packhorses. It appeared that they were being forced to carry the baggage and supplies that had been unloaded from the wagons to make space for wounded men.

There were hundreds of prisoners, more than Broken Trail could count. In this multitude he had to find one young, brown-haired redcoat, possibly without a cap. The best way to do it, he decided, was to station himself at a vantage point ahead of the army's advance—at a spot where he could see but not be seen while scrutinizing each face as the prisoners passed.

Moving at double the army's speed, he found a hiding place that the army would have to pass on its way. It was a leafy thicket from which he had a clear view of the track.

He had only a short time to wait before the front of the army drew level with his hiding place. At the head were the officers, riding their horses at an easy walk. Though the uniforms of some looked the worse for wear, and one horse had a patch of dried blood on its flank, the officers made a brave show. There were some fine-looking horses, too. Now that he had mastered the knack of managing a horse, Broken Trail would have liked one of those for himself. The most handsome was a grey gelding ridden by an extremely fat officer. That must be Major Ferguson's horse, he thought, remembering the remarks of the Over Mountain men. Somebody named Cleveland had claimed Major Ferguson's horse. "You could make two Pat Fergusons out of a man that size," one of the Over Mountain men had said. Yet the grey gelding stepped along as smartly as if it carried a feather on its back. With its thick, arched neck and flowing mane, that horse looked like a chief, born to lead.

Following the officers were ranks of blue-coated soldiers. After them came the prisoners and their guards. Broken Trail recognized Major Ferguson's aide, Captain DePeyster. Even on foot, he kept his high and mighty air, marching with his shoulders square and his chin up. He still wore his white wig and tricorn hat, but not his sword.

Farther along the line, Broken Trail saw the soldier with broken teeth. He looked much different now that he had been deprived of his musket. His back was bowed with the weight of a large bundle draped across his shoulders.

The army passed like a slow-flowing river. One wounded

redcoat collapsed as Broken Trail watched. Promptly, two guards dragged him off the track and left him lying face down in the mud.

Then Broken Trail saw Elijah. Though his face was begrimed with gunpowder, there was no mistaking who he was. Bare-headed, he walked with his left arm hanging useless at his side. There was a slash in the left shoulder of his scarlet coat, and around the slash a darker stain. Staring straight ahead, he looked like someone walking in his sleep.

The man on Elijah's left and the man on his right both bore heavy loads. Yet it was Elijah, carrying nothing, who faltered with every step. Maybe it was loss of blood that weakened him. Or hunger. Or both. He looked very thin. Tall and thin. Three years ago, he had not been nearly so tall.

He was alive and he could walk! Broken Trail offered a quick prayer of thanks to the Great Spirit, and then a second prayer for help to set Elijah free.

At first the track ran through a forest of maples and yellow birch. Then gradually the woods gave way to small farms, where homesteaders had built their log cabins and cleared patches of land.

With no trees close to the track to hide behind, Broken Trail climbed up into the wooded hills above the farms. Here he was well hidden, but still had a good view of the army's movement along the track. As he walked along, keeping pace with the army, he kept an eye on Elijah's place in the column, just in case he fell and was abandoned along the way.

Shortly before sunset the army stopped at the entrance to a farm lane. The creaking wagons fell silent, the weary horses hauling them sagged in their harnesses, and the exhausted prisoners were finally allowed to sit down.

The farm where the army stopped was not a humble homestead like the others they had passed. This one boasted a big, white house with many windows, two chimneys and wide stone steps leading up to a huge front door. Behind the house were a long, low building, a barn and a silo. The farm included ploughed fields, orchards and broad pasturelands enclosed by a snake fence.

Broken Trail saw black men trudging in from the fields carrying hoes over their shoulders while white men looked on. The black men filed into the long, low building. When all were inside, a white man locked the door. There were about twenty black men, and only four white. Why, Broken Trail wondered, did the black men put up with this treatment? Since they outnumbered the white men, why didn't they lock *them* up?

At the head of the army, the officers appeared to be conferring. Still mounted, they looked toward the house. The officer with the most gold braid seemed to be doing the talking. The others nodded. At length it appeared that something had been decided. Two officers turned their horses and, leaving the others, trotted briskly up to the house.

After a few minutes, they cantered back. They pointed toward the pasture. The army began to move again, heading slowly along the lane. Halfway to the house, it turned left through an open gate into the pasture, and there it came to a halt.

Flat and level at the top, the pasture sloped gently toward creek flats, where a stream ran through. Part of the pasture-land had been cleared, but some was still in bush. Down at the creek flats, the grass was lush and green.

Broken Trail watched from the hillside to see what would happen next.

When the officers' horses had been unsaddled and the draught horses unharnessed, the fat officer pointed toward the stream at the lower end of the pasture. Promptly, six soldiers stepped forward. One grasped the halter of the grey horse. The other five were close behind as he led it down the slope. With no urging, the herd followed. Broken Trail counted thirty horses ambling to the part of the pasture where the greenest grass grew. After hobbling the horses, the soldiers rejoined the other men, leaving no guard.

Broken Trail knew in a flash exactly what he was going to do.

Making a wide detour of the farm, he approached the pasture from the woods on the far side. He crept up to the snake fence. Peering between the rails, he could see everything.

Some soldiers were pitching tents. Others were herding the prisoners together, encircling them with a ring of guards. With so many prisoners crowded together, it took Broken Trail a long time locate Elijah. His heart lifted when he spotted him close to the edge of the mass of prisoners. Although he did not like the way his brother sank wearily to the ground, it was a relief to know where he could find him when the right moment came.

As Broken Trail settled down to wait, fires were lit and cauldrons were hung on tripods above the flames. He was close enough to see steam rising from the food in the big cooking pots, but not close enough to smell it. He wondered what the army would eat for supper. Remembering the goodness of pork and beans simmered with molasses, he sighed as he pulled a hardtack from the bag at his belt.

Soldiers holding metal bowls lined up for food while the prisoners watched. From the dispirited way they slumped, Broken Trail reckoned they knew that the steaming contents of the cooking pots were not for them.

Darkness fell and quiet settled upon the camp. At the bottom of the pasture, the horses stopped grazing and dozed.

The time had come. Broken Trail crept under the bottom rail of the fence and moved at a crouch toward the horses. As he neared them, he dropped to the ground and crawled. He knew the danger. No one could predict what horses would do if disturbed in the middle of the night. Instinct might tell them that the creature creeping through the grass was a cougar. If they panicked, he would have thirty sets of pounding hooves around him.

"*Oki*, help me," he muttered. What wouldn't he give for a whiff of wolverine!

The horses did not panic. Their bellies full, they rested quietly. When Broken Trail's knife severed the hobbles of the first horse, its only reaction was to paw the ground. The second gave a low snort. Did horses dream? he wondered. He freed another horse and then another from its hobbles. Most seemed too drowsy to notice that their legs were no longer tied.

He left the grey gelding for last. At once, he saw a difference. This horse was wide awake. Nickering softly while he cut the rope, it bent that noble arching neck to gaze at him. Its ears were pricked forward, and its large eyes were luminous. He wished that he knew its name.

Broken Trail stood up and faced the grey horse. He scratched the skin between its eyes and ran his hands along its neck. From his pouch he pulled out the cord that Red Sun Rising had given him to steer the horse he had ridden to Kings Mountain. He slipped the loop of the cord around the grey's lower jaw. Whispering gently, he leaned against its withers and with a smooth leap laid his body across its back. The horse's muscles tightened. Then he threw a leg over, steadied himself, and gripped tight with his calves.

"Are you ready?" he whispered.

The grey stamped its front hooves.

Broken Trail sucked in all the air his lungs could hold. Then he raised his head. Holding his open palm to his mouth to block the intervals of sound, he gave the high, yelping whoop of the Oneida war cry. The grey horse bucked.

On all sides, wild whinnies filled the air. At a slap on the rump, the grey bounded forward. With pounding hooves, the others surged after it. Thirty horses careening through the night.

Chapter 12

BROKEN TRAIL LAY FORWARD along the grey's neck, its mane sweeping his face. If he fell off, the following horses would trample him. But he felt no fear. This was like flying, like being borne aloft on an eagle's wings. The snake fence caught his eye. For a moment, he thought the horse would jump; but when he pulled on the cord, it veered away.

One gallop around the pasture, and then he directed the horse through the open gate and down the lane. The herd followed. On reaching the track, he slowed his horse to a canter, and then to a soft trot. The game was over.

Bringing the grey to a halt, he stroked its neck. "Good boy!"

He slid from its back. Leaving the herd scattered up and down the track, he raced to the camp. Chaos was everywhere. Soldiers were running after the horses. Prisoners, left unguarded, were seizing the chance to escape.

"Cherokees!" someone yelled. "Damned horse thieves."

Cherokees! Broken Trail laughed.

But the joke would be on him if the rebels were to capture him wearing his deerskin clothes. Trusting to the darkness and the turmoil to escape notice, he raced to the upper part of the pasture. Their guards gone, few prisoners remained. But Elijah had not moved. There he sat, almost alone, his shoulders slumped and his head bent. Only when Broken Trail dropped to his knees beside him did Elijah slowly turn his head.

"You." His eyes brightened. "Moses. It *was* you."

"Yes." For now at least, Elijah was welcome to use the old name.

"How did you get here?"

"I followed the army. Come on. Let's go!"

"I don't have the strength to go anywhere."

Broken Trail tugged at his arm. "Yes, you do. I'm not leaving you here."

Elijah shook his had. "You can't help me."

But he must have seen something in Broken Trail's face. The hardness. The determination. Elijah took the hand held out to him and let Broken Trail haul him to his feet. Glancing in the direction of the track, Broken Trail saw the grey horse being led by its halter. Soon the roundup would be complete, and then the soldiers would go after the escaping prisoners. There was no time to lose.

Broken Trail pulled Elijah's uninjured arm over his shoulder. Somehow, they ran.

After the burst of speed that took them from the camp and onto the track, Elijah had no strength left. The farm was barely out of sight when his legs collapsed under him. He gave out a long groan and, as he fell, pulled Broken Trail down with him.

"We must keep going," Broken Trail said. They sat side by side in the mud.

"Where?"

"Back to Kings Mountain."

"God forbid!" Elijah's voice cracked.

"Not to the battlefield. Below the hill there's a place to hide." He peered at Elijah's shoulder. The waning moon gave enough light for Broken Trail to see the slash in his brother's tunic. "That hole in your coat doesn't look like a bullet made it."

"It was a bayonet."

"That's the worst kind. It means the wound's full of dirt and bits of cloth." Broken Trail paused, thinking of the clean water in the stream near the base of Kings Mountain. "We must keep moving."

"I can't walk all the way back to Kings Mountain. It's sixteen miles. I heard an officer say, 'Sixteen miles from Kings Mountain to Waldron's plantation.' That's what he called the farm where the army pitched camp."

For Broken Trail, sixteen miles was nothing. For Elijah, it might as well be one thousand. But it was certain that he and Elijah could not stay here, where homesteaders' cabins dotted the clearings along the track.

"There's a forest not too far ahead." He stood up. "Then we can rest."

"You never give up, do you?" Elijah grasped the hand held out to him, struggled to his feet, and wrapped his arm around the smaller boy's shoulder.

Taking Elijah's weight, Broken Trail stumbled at his first step, barely recovering his balance. He took a second step, and then a third. Pain throbbed in his neck.

Careful not to trip in the deep ruts, he kept his eyes on the track ahead of him. Only once in a while did he raise his head to estimate their progress. They passed clearings, small woodlots, barns and log cabins. It felt like an eternity before they reached the forest.

Practically carrying Elijah, Broken Trail left the track and entered the woods. Pushing through bushes and stumbling over uneven ground, he kept going until they came upon an open patch under a big tree. Broken Trail's neck felt ready to break. He could support Elijah no farther.

Almost as soon as Broken Trail had lowered him to the ground, Elijah fell into a state resembling sleep. It was not normal sleep. His eyes twitched. He mumbled and cried out as if in the grip of a terrible nightmare. Sitting beside him and holding both his hands, Broken Trail shivered at the sound of his laboured breathing, for each intake of breath was a groan and each exhalation a hoarse whistle. He may not live through the night, Broken Trail thought. Elijah's moaning sounded like a death song to his ears.

A wind sprang up. Clouds covered the moon, and a cold drizzle began to fall. The dried blood on Elijah's coat softened, becoming sticky to the touch.

Elijah's breathing changed. He gasped and gulped for air. Broken Trail squeezed his hands, leaned over him, and whispered in his ear, "Don't leave me. I need you." He wanted to say, *I love you*, which was what he meant.

In response, Elijah's whole body gave a terrible jerk. Then his breathing became quieter and the moaning began again. Broken Trail watched through the night, listening to his brother's every breath.

Chapter 13

AROUND MIDDAY THEY reached the maple tree at the foot of Kings Mountain. Broken Trail pulled aside the vines that covered the entrance to the washout cavity.

"In there," he said.

Elijah stared. "It's a hole in the ground!"

"It's dry and it's safe."

"How do I get in?"

"Wriggle in feet first. I reckon you can't crawl very well with your shoulder hurt."

Inside, there was scarcely room to move. Elijah, flat on his back, took up most of the space, leaving Broken Trail huddled with his head touching the exposed roots that formed the rough roof.

Elijah's pewter buttons glinted in the faint light that penetrated the vines. Leaning over, Broken Trail unfastened the top button, and then the next.

"What are you doing?" Elijah asked.

"I need to look at your wound."

Elijah lay unresisting while the rest of the buttons were unfastened, wincing only when his linsey-woolsey undershirt was pulled from his skin. Even though it had been softened by rain, the congealed blood stuck like glue.

The wound was in the soft spot just inside the upper part of his arm. There was no fresh bleeding, just milky seepage and pus. Around the gash, the flesh was hot and swollen. An abscess. That was no surprise.

What did surprise Broken Trail was the Iroquois medicine bag that hung on a leather thong around his brother's neck. It was a tiny bag, brightly painted with many symbols. He touched it reverently. How did a white soldier come to possess so sacred an object? It meant that the unseen spirits were protecting Elijah. But why should this be? What story lay behind it? Now was not the right time to ask.

He said, "You need a poultice on your wound."

"A poultice! Where are we going to find a poultice around here?"

"I can make one. I just have to mash up the inner bark from a slippery elm. There's some growing nearby. And there's white willow, too. Soaking white willow bark in water makes a drink that lessens pain." He found himself taking pride in showing off his knowledge. "That's the sort of thing every Oneida knows about."

"Do what you can." Elijah's forehead was beaded with sweat, and his eyes had a glazed look when they met Broken Trail's.

Broken Trail unhooked the canteen from Elijah's belt and crawled from the hole. The steep side of Kings Mountain loomed over his shoulder as he walked down to the creek. In this glade he and Red Sun Rising had left the horses hobbled while they went to give the message to Major Ferguson. Was that only two days ago? It felt twice that long. Now little piles of horse manure were the only evidence of horses having been there.

Broken Trail had told Red Sun Rising to take one of the horses and to leave the other for him. Travelling on horseback, Red Sun Rising must be nearly home by now. What a warm welcome awaited him! Broken Trail pictured him riding into Chickamauga wearing the handsome red coat and riding the dark horse.

What had become of the second horse? Broken Trail wondered. Most likely an Over Mountain man had come upon it, cut the hobbles and ridden off. A fine prize to take home!

On the flood plain Broken Trail quickly found a large slippery elm from which he could strip bark without killing the tree. He knew the rituals for gathering medicines. It was not only animals that had spirits. Shrubs, herbs and trees all must be spoken to before their parts could be harvested. Standing at the foot of the tree, he chanted softly:

> Share with me your power to cleanse and to heal.
> Pardon me that I have no sacrifice to offer,
> No wampum or tobacco or beads.
> My thanks are all I can give in return for your gift.
> It is for my brother that I need your healing power.

With the blade of his tomahawk he hacked through the furrowed outer bark of the slippery elm, and then used his knife to cut away the sticky, slippery inner bark. When he had enough to make a poultice, he wrapped it in burdock leaves.

Broken Trail chanted the same words to the white willow that he found growing beside the creek. He needed only a little of its inner bark, just enough to trim into slender strips that would go through the opening of Elijah's canteen to steep in fresh water from the creek.

Finally, he found rocks of the right size and shape to serve as a natural mortar and pestle. When he had pounded the slippery elm bark to a thick paste, he carried it in burdock leaves to the cavity under the maple tree.

Taking care of Elijah gave Broken Trail a good feeling. It seemed as though the two of them had crammed into one day and one night three lost years of brotherhood. Before long, they would have to part again; he tried not to think about that.

When Broken Trail had laid the wet poultice on the wound and covered it with the burdock leaves, Elijah looked more cheerful. Without objection, he drank the sour liquid in his canteen.

"The drink will make you feel better soon," Broken Trail said. "The poultice takes longer. By tomorrow we'll see a difference."

Elijah smiled weakly. "You should be a doctor."

Broken Trail shrugged. He saw himself as a future warrior, not as a healer—though both deserved respect.

"I mean it. You could teach a few things to that sawbones of a surgeon in our regiment. After every battle, he inspects our wounded. Shot in the leg? Cut it off. Shot in the arm? Cut it off. Shot in the head? Cut—"

Broken Trail laughed. "Oneida healing is different. We know how to draw out poisons. In our villages, you don't see many old warriors hobbling around with limbs missing."

That night Broken Trail slept sitting up, his legs bent and his head slumped on his knees. Too uncomfortable to slumber long, he woke in the middle of the night and, unable to fall asleep again, pondered the strange turn his life had taken. More and more he came to believe that finding Elijah was part of the Great Spirit's plan. But what purpose lay behind it?

He knew about men and women whom the unseen spirits

had especially favoured. Some, like Wolf Woman, had a gift for healing. Some had power to find things that were lost. Some had the power to know what they did not know. To him, this was the most mysterious gift of all. How could you know what you did not know? Yet it was this power that he sometimes felt stirring within him, giving him an unsettling feeling, like being helpless and powerful at the same time.

Sensing Elijah's eyes on him, he turned his head. It was too dark to distinguish his brother's face.

"You awake, too?" Elijah said.

"I can't sleep. I've been thinking about everything that's happened, like finding you, and what it all means."

"I always thought we would meet again. After you ran away, I never stopped wondering what became of you."

"That's a long story."

"Reckon it must be." He hesitated. "Tell me about it. Start where the Oneidas carried you off. What did they do with you?"

"They adopted me to replace a boy who'd died. My new mother's brother became my teacher. That's the Oneida way. I was nearly ten, and I knew nothing that an Oneida boy that age should know."

Once Broken Trail started talking, he found it easy to go on. He described how the Oneidas had brought him up as one of their own, although some rejected him. He found himself opening up to Elijah about his fears, about how long he had waited for his *oki*, his totem animal, to appear and how terrible it had been when the vision of his future was snatched away at the last moment. Then he described how the two soldiers had taken him to their camp, where the captain had promised him a rifle as payment for delivering the warning to Major Ferguson.

Elijah listened with complete attention, asking a question now and then, as if determined to understand. When Broken Trail had finished, he asked, "Do you reckon your *oki* will come back someday to let you see that vision?"

"As soon as I return to my village, I'll ask my uncle about that. He's very wise about such matters." He paused. "Now tell me your story."

"I'll start where you did. We were camped by Oneida Lake with two Mohawk warriors to protect us."

"Axe Carrier and Okwaho."

"Yes. Okwaho was my hero. You were jealous when he took me hunting."

"Can you blame me? Back in Canajoharie, we used to do everything together. You taught me to fish. You promised that you would take me hunting as soon as I was old enough. But after Okwaho took you under his wing, you had no time for me." He paused. "And then Ma made me gather nuts with the little girls. That was more than I could bear."

"Ma blamed me when you ran away. I would have run away too, but Okwaho wouldn't take me with him. 'My path not good path for you,' he told me. That nearly broke my heart. But then he gave me a medicine bag."

"I saw it."

"I never take it off. Okwaho promised it would keep me safe. There's a stone the colour of blood inside, and dust made from the skin of a rattlesnake and the beak of an eagle."

"Powerful medicine," Broken Trail said. "Hundreds of soldiers died on Kings Mountain, but you're alive."

"It was Okwaho who turned me into a sharp shooter. You might say, it's because of him I'm here today."

"I remember how he hung a dead squirrel high up in a pine tree and made you keep trying until your arrow hit it."

"He was a good teacher. When I joined the Royal Greens, I was the only recruit who could hit a blessed thing with those muskets they issued. That's why Major Ferguson picked me for his rifle company. Ferguson invented a new kind of rifle, a breech-loader. Very fast. I figure he was the smartest man in the world . . . except he got a lot of us killed."

"That wasn't too smart."

"Well, he didn't know how to fight in the mountains. We were sitting ducks. But he wouldn't budge. He told the men, 'I'm on Kings Mountain and I'm the king of that mountain. God Almighty and all the rebels of Hell can't drive me from it.'"

"The British sent me to warn him. I arrived in time, but I never had a chance to deliver my message. The soldiers wouldn't listen. They mocked me."

"It wouldn't have made any difference if you had given your message to Major Ferguson. He had already decided to make a stand on Kings Mountain while we waited for reinforcements. Once he made up his mind, nothing could change it."

"I saw what happened. I was hiding with my friend in a clump of junipers on the hillside when the rebels sneaked up. They had good cover behind the trees."

"On the plateau we had no cover. We had to go out in the open to shoot. When we fired down the hill, our shots went above the rebels' heads. They charged over the top and mowed us down. Ferguson was on his horse, wearing that checkered hunting shirt over his uniform, galloping all over the battlefield, blowing his silver whistle."

"I heard the whistle."

"After he fell, we tried to surrender. Two of our men went out waving white flags. The rebels shot them down. When we raised the white flag again, they finally stopped shooting. They told us to lay down our weapons and sit on the ground. As soon as those Over Mountain men saw us sitting there defenceless, they went crazy. They're devils, not men. Even the regular soldiers were out of control. They stripped Major Ferguson naked, along with Virginia Sal, and threw them into the same grave. While all this was going on, I lay on the ground and played dead. I'd had one bayonet stuck in me already and didn't want another."

"I heard them yell, 'Remember Waxhaws!' What did that mean?"

"Waxhaws is where Banastre Tarleton's troops massacred rebel soldiers who were trying to surrender. That's what they say. Major Ferguson's men weren't there. Whatever happened, we never did it." He shook his head. "You say you were hiding with your friend. Who was he? What happened to him?"

"He's a Cherokee, and he guided me to Kings Mountain. His name is Red Sun Rising. Nothing happened to him—I mean, he wasn't killed. He left for home the morning after the battle. I reckon he's back in Chickamauga by now."

"Chickamauga! That's where the diehards live. Dragging Canoe and his warriors are ready to fight to the last man rather than give up one more inch of their land."

"Red Sun Rising is ready to die with them."

"If we'd had some of those Chickamauga Cherokees fighting alongside the Loyal Americans, the last campaign might have ended differently."

"They could have taught Major Ferguson how to fight in the mountains . . . supposing he would listen. Red Sun Rising said the Loyal Americans were making a big mistake if they thought no one could defeat them on Kings Mountain. And he said that *before* the battle."

"Turns out he was right."

In his mind Broken Trail he saw the bodies lying on the battlefield and the wounded being marched away. He said, "I went to Kings Mountain because I wanted a rifle, but I found my brother instead. That's the one good thing that came of it."

Silence fell. From Elijah's steady breathing Broken Trail realized that he had slipped into a quiet, restful sleep.

Chapter 14

IN THE MORNING Broken Trail took Elijah's undershirt and coat to the stream and washed them in the clear water, pounding them on a rock to remove every bit of blood. After bringing them back to the maple tree, he draped them over a bush to dry, close enough to the cavity's entrance that he could pull them inside if he heard anyone approach. That scarlet coat with its blue facings made a brilliant contrast to the bush's grey-green leaves.

Then he changed the poultice. Already it was doing its work, pulling out not only pus but also bits of dirt and shreds of fabric that the bayonet had driven into the wound. The swelling was down. Elijah's brow was cool.

Elijah slept most of the day, waking only to eat and drink.

After trying both hardtack and corn powder, Elijah said he would leave the corn powder for Broken Trail, explaining that he was happy with hardtack, being used to it. Broken Trail was glad to learn that.

The following morning, the swelling was almost gone. "You're well enough to travel," Broken Trail said as he washed the skin around the wound, "if you take it slowly."

"Good. After three days in a burrow, I'm starting to feel like a badger."

"We've been safe under this tree. I don't know anything about the folks who live nearby, but they aren't likely to be friendly."

"My uniform may be a problem. Anybody can spot my red coat a mile away."

"You could rub it with mud."

"Oh, no!" Elijah looked shocked. But then he shrugged. "My coat will be filthy anyway by the time I've waded through the swamps to Charleston."

"Charleston? Where's that?"

"About a hundred miles southeast from here."

"Why do you have to go there?"

"To report for duty. Charleston is the centre for British military operations in the south."

"Oh." For a moment, Broken Trail had nothing to say. He must go north. Elijah must go south. They might never meet again.

"What about you?" Elijah asked.

"I'm going back to my village. Nobody knows what's become of me. I don't know what kind of welcome I'll receive. The longer I'm away, the worse it will be."

"So you're heading back to Oneida Lake."

"No. Not there. Over a year ago, the rebels drove us from those lands. My band's new village is on the north shore of the St. Lawrence River, one day's paddle east of Carleton Island."

"Carleton Island! Is that right?" Elijah fell silent. He lay on his back, staring straight up at the spider webs above his head. After a long time had passed, he said: "I'll go with you as far as Carleton Island."

"Go with me?" Broken Trail pondered this. Nothing could please him more than to travel on a long trail with his brother, yet he suppressed the thrill of gladness that rose in him. Elijah had disappointed him in the past. He must not let it happen again. "You just told me you have to report for duty," he said brusquely.

"I do. But Fort Haldimand on Carleton Island is where I joined the Royal Greens. Why shouldn't I go back there to report for duty? It's where I enlisted in the first place."

"Isn't Carleton Island a lot farther off than Charleston?"

"Five times farther." Another pause. "Truth is, it will give you and me a chance to catch up."

"Makes sense to me." Broken Trail cleared his throat, still hiding his eagerness. "Besides, I'm not sure you're strong enough yet to travel on your own."

Elijah may not have been listening. He appeared to be lost in his own thoughts.

"If we go to Carleton Island," he said, "we can see Ma and Hope."

"You can see them, not me. They're not my family any more. Not since the Oneidas adopted me."

"But Ma is still the mother that gave you birth. And Hope is still your little sister. You can't change that."

"Yes, I can!" Broken Trail sat up so quickly he bumped his head hard on the underside of a root as thick as a man's torso. "I have an Oneida family now."

"Just a minute. If the first nine years of your life count for nothing, then what are you doing here with me?"

Broken Trail did not answer. It was something he could not explain. He had tried so hard to forget Elijah. It was his duty to forget him. But even on his dream quest, while he was fasting in the wilderness waiting for his vision, it had been Elijah's face that he saw when he looked at his own reflection in the pool of quiet water.

"Are you telling me I'll always be white at heart? That's what my enemies think. Is that what you think, too?"

"I'm not saying that." Elijah spoke slowly, as if weighing every word. "You reckon you have to be one or the other, either white or Oneida. But it doesn't need to be that way."

"Yes, it does." Broken Trail scowled. "A man can't follow two paths at the same time. He has to make a choice."

Elijah sat up and lightly punched Broken Trail's shoulder.

"Sorry if I said the wrong thing. I don't want to quarrel. Let's go. We have a long journey ahead."

Broken Trail was glad to drop the subject. Elijah put troubling thoughts into his head. Could Carries a Quiver, so wise about many things, be wrong about this?

They crawled out of the hole. Elijah blinked when the sunshine struck his face. When he stood, he had to rest one hand against the tree trunk to steady himself. He shook his head. "Don't worry. I'll be fine."

Broken Trail could not say the same for himself. He tried to fix his mind on his Oneida home and on his duty, but found that he could no longer see so clearly what that duty was.

Chapter 15

FOR THE FIRST FOUR days of their journey, everything looked different. Perhaps on his way south, too much of his effort had been directed to staying on the horse and not enough to noticing landmarks that any warrior should automatically store in his memory. Whatever the reason, Broken Trail could not shake off the uncomfortable feeling that he had lost his way.

It was not until the fifth day, when they reached the farm where he and Red Sun Rising had stolen the horses, that Broken Trail knew exactly where he was.

Although it had been night when he saw it the first time,

he recognized the farm at once. It stood nestled in the hills, just off the main trail. There was the two-storey home built of dressed timber, the barn, the paddock and the small log outbuilding. A flock of brown hens with bright red combs, scrabbling for scattered grain near the open door of the outbuilding, made clear its present use. That hen house must have been the family's original log cabin, Broken Trail thought, for not only was it larger than a chicken coop needed to be, but it boasted a big stone chimney and, in one sidewall, a window. The window was boarded over. Although some chinking was missing from between the logs, the chicken house was still a sturdy-looking building.

There were also pigs on the farm, not in a pen but branded and ranging free. The only fence was the one around the empty paddock.

Seeing the paddock, Broken Trail felt a twinge of guilt. Maybe the farmer had not had time to replace the horses that Broken Trail and Red Sun Rising had stolen. Or maybe he could not afford to.

"You've stopped walking." Elijah's voice interrupted his thoughts.

"Have I?"

"And you're looking mighty hard at that farm."

"This is where Red Sun Rising and I stole the horses."

"I wish we had those horses now!"

Broken Trail gulped. "I wish we did too, so I could give them back. Red Sun Rising said it was right to take them because white settlers stole Cherokee land. But it didn't feel right to me."

"What's right doesn't matter. In a war, people have to take what they need."

He started to walk on, but Broken Trail did not move.

"Look!" he said. "There's a girl."

A girl wearing a grey gown and a white apron had come from the house. Her hair was in two long, brown braids. She looked about twelve years old.

Elijah stopped. He looked, too.

"Sure enough," he laughed. "That's a girl. Haven't you ever seen one before?"

"Shh!"

The girl looked around, but not in their direction.

"Come, Rover!" she called. "Time to round up the chickens." Her voice was clear and sweet, with a twang.

A shaggy black and white dog rose from a patch of sunshine and shook itself.

"I remember that dog," Broken Trail said. "Red Sun Rising fed it a charm so it wouldn't bark."

"It looks to me like your eyes are more on the girl than on the dog." Elijah grinned. Then his expression changed, and in an instant he was serious. "If you want to watch, we'd better hide. We don't want the folks living here to see us."

"You're right. With me in deerskins and you in a red coat, we wouldn't enjoy the welcome they'd give us."

Ducking out of sight, they crawled through the bushes to

a honeysuckle thicket where they could see without being seen.

"Rover, go get 'em!" The girl stuck her fingers into her mouth and whistled. That's all she had to do. Running close to the ground, the dog made a wide circle around the chickens. Clucking indignantly, but not overly alarmed, they moved in closer together. Then the dog completed a second, tighter circle that manoeuvred them right through the coop's open door. The girl, close behind, slammed it shut. The dog trotted to her side.

"Good dog!" She reached down to rub its ear.

"Well, I never!" Elijah whispered. "That girl didn't have to lift a finger except to shut the door. That's a smart dog."

"The girl's the smart one—getting the dog to do all the work."

A woman came from the house. She wore a white mobcap on her head, and a grey homespun dress very like the girl's.

"Libby dear, you and Rover better drive the hogs into the barn before your pa and your brother arrive home with those new horses. I don't want them spooked by hogs before they get used to this place."

"Yes, Ma." She turned to the dog. "Pigs, Rover!"

"Seen enough?" Elijah asked.

"No. I want to see the horses."

"We don't know how long we'd have to wait. And it's not safe—"

"Shh!" Broken Trail raised his hand. "Listen."

Hoof beats.

There was no time to look for a safer hiding place. Broken Trail and Elijah lay still, their bodies pressed to the ground and only their heads held up to see what was happening.

Turning off the main trail were two horsemen. One horse was a roan gelding, and the other a bay mare.

The man riding the gelding was middle-aged and completely bald, with a brown beard so bushy that it more than made up for the absence of hair on top of his head. The other man was much younger, about eighteen years old. His blond hair was cut short, and he had a corn-coloured crop of chin whiskers.

The men rode their horses straight through the open gate into the paddock. Before they had dismounted, the woman walked over and rested her arms on the top rail.

"They look good, Judah," she said. "Let's hope Cherokees don't steal them, too."

"Laura, I have some mighty good news," the older man said in a deep, rumbling voice. "Today there's one less murdering horse thief roaming the hills."

"Don't tell me Captain Cherokee has been caught!"

"The very same."

"Some fellows spotted him trying to steal a horse over near Tar Heel," the younger man said as he dismounted. "He was easy enough for them to spot, wearing that red coat with all the gold trim."

"All dressed up for a party!" the man called Judah rumbled. "A hanging party, that is. Laura, I hope y'all got plenty of flour and eggs on hand. There'll be a crowd here for breakfast tomorrow. Nothing like watching a hanging to give a man a good appetite."

"The Lord be thanked!" the woman exclaimed. "I ain't felt safe for one minute since he butchered that family over by Elizabethtown. What kind of monster would kill an innocent baby? And those two sweet little girls."

Broken Trail nudged Elijah's arm. He whispered in his ear. "They're talking about Red Sun Rising. He took a uniform from a dead officer on the battlefield at Kings Mountain. I saw him strutting around in it. But they've got one thing wrong. He didn't kill that family. No, sir! We were travelling together when we came upon those folks. They were dead already."

Judah was still talking. "Some of the boys are bringing him in. They'll be here by sundown. We'll lock Captain Cherokee in the chicken house tonight, then hang him first thing in the morning."

"We should hang him just as soon as they bring him in," the younger man said. "Why wait?"

"What! Cheat good folks out of the pleasure of watching him die? Half the homesteaders in Watauga County have been attacked by savages claiming to own this land. People will come from miles around to see him hang."

"You unsaddle the horses and take the tack into the barn,"

the woman said to the younger man. "Give Libby a hand with the pigs. Then both of you come in for supper."

As soon as the whole family was in the house, Broken Trail sat up. "We have to rescue him," he said.

"How?"

"I don't know yet. We need a plan. But first, we need a better place to hide."

Elijah pointed to a stand of sumac a little way up the side of the nearest hill. The sumacs' green leaves were splashed with crimson. "What about there?"

Broken Trail nodded. "The leaves are the same colour as your coat. Nobody will notice us there. And it's close enough for us to hear and see what's happening."

They slipped through the trees around the perimeter of the farm and up the hill to the sumac stand. They settled down to wait. Elijah munched a hardtack biscuit. Broken Trail ate a bit of corn powder, followed by water from Elijah's flask.

Laughter was what they heard first, followed by hoof beats. A few moments later five horsemen came into sight around a bend in the trail. With them was a sixth horse, led by a rope tied to its halter. Slung across this horse's back was a man, bound hand and foot. Broken Trail recognized the scarlet coat, the deerskin leggings and the three feathers that dangled from the prisoner's scalp lock.

"That's him," Broken Trail said, "Red Sun Rising."

"Hey, Judah!" One of the riders called out. "We brought you a guest."

Judah emerged from the house. "Throw him in the chicken coop. And stick a gag in his mouth. I don't want the hens upset. It puts them off laying. When you're done, I'll put a padlock on the door."

"Here's what we'll do," Broken Trail whispered as he watched the men carry Red Sun Rising into the chicken house. "After it's dark, you stay here to keep watch while I creep down the hill, pull the boards from the chicken house window, and crawl inside. After I've cut his ropes, Red Sun Rising and I can climb back out the window."

"You know what I think? I think you'll get yourself hanged along with your friend. They're sure to set guards on the chicken house all night long."

"Sooner or later, guards doze off. That's why war parties always attack just before dawn."

"What about the dog? He'll wake them with his barking."

"Hardtack will take care of Rover. He's not a keen watchdog."

The sound of hoof beats rose toward them.

Elijah whispered. "More men coming. Keep your head down."

Four horsemen made up the next group. Close behind came a dozen more.

"They brought their own supplies," Elijah whispered.

"What?"

"Those horses are carrying enough casks of rum to get a regiment drunk."

"Good," Broken Trail said.

Soon a bonfire blazed in the middle of the farmyard. More horsemen arrived. They all carried rifles, and most brought stoneware jugs as well. Broken Trail counted twenty-two men. Over their everyday clothes, some wore the long, white shirts that were their battledress.

At an upstairs window, the young girl set a lighted candle on the windowsill. Broken Trail was glad to see that she was safely out of the way of the men. Downstairs, the girl's mother occasionally passed in front of the kitchen window, the glow of the cooking fire behind her. She had a purposeful walk, as if she were on guard to protect her home.

In the barnyard, men milled about the bonfire. Buoyed by drink, they hollered and cheered. Broken Trail's heart raced as he heard their mingled shouts: "Bring the savage out!" "Hand 'im over!" "We'll take care of this." "Hang the killer now."

Judah, who seemed to be the only man not drinking, jumped onto the flatbed of an empty hay wagon. "No!" he thundered. "More folks are coming in the morning. They'll feel robbed if we don't wait till then."

The paddock was crammed with horses. Ears flattened, they stamped their hooves, snorted, and whinnied restlessly.

Looking toward the chicken house, Broken Trail imagined Red Sun Rising lying on a dirt floor, tied hand and foot amid chicken droppings and dirty feathers, surrounded by cackling hens.

Chapter 16

TWO MEN WEARING long white shirts sat on the ground a few yards from the chicken house door, their backs against a tree stump and their rifles lying beside their outstretched legs. Back and forth between them they passed a stoneware jug, from which each drank deeply at his turn.

As for the dog, it slunk about with its tail drooping, sniffing at men's legs.

"Rover is off duty tonight," Elijah whispered. "We won't need to waste any hardtack on him."

"They all look like they're off duty."

"If they keep up the drinking, there won't be a man on his feet by morning."

Around the bonfire, the mood had changed from anger to sociability. The shouts for vengeance ceased. Having made themselves comfortable, the men appeared ready to enjoy their vigil. Someone began to sing:

Yankee Doodle went to town
A-riding on a pony
Stuck a feather in his hat
And called it macaroni.

Others took up the chorus:

Yankee Doodle, keep it up
Yankee Doodle dandy
Mind the music and the step
And with the girls be handy.

It was a lively tune. Broken Trail found his toe tapping. The singer launched into the second verse:

Father and I went down to camp
Along with Captain Gooding
And there we saw the men and boys
As thick as hasty pudding.

"What's it about?" Broken Trail whispered.

Elijah scowled. "Joining the rebel army. Bunch of scoundrels!"

There was General Washington
Upon a slapping stallion

A-giving orders to his men
I guess there was a million.

"I know about him," Broken Trail said. "It was Washington that gave the orders for every Iroquois town to be burned. That's how we lost our land, even though the Oneidas were helping the rebels."

"They even stole that tune," Elijah muttered, "and put their own words to it."

Yankee Doodle, keep it up
Yankee Doodle dandy
Mind the music and the step
And with the girls be handy.

"It's a good song anyway," Broken Trail said when it ended. "I hope they give us another to pass the time."

But there would be no encore. The men around the fire began to tell stories. From the sudden bursts of laughter Broken Trail thought they must be jokes. He was not close enough to hear them, and figured he wouldn't understand them anyway.

Occasionally a man left the group, wandered off unsteadily into the shadows, and then returned. Gradually the voices died down. It seemed that most of the men had fallen asleep where they lay.

There was only a sliver of a moon. The flames of the bonfire burned low, and their flickering light no longer reached as far as the chicken house. Broken Trail could hardly see the two guards, but he did not think they had moved.

He leaned toward Elijah. “I’m going down to the chicken coop.”

“Too soon.”

“I’ll lie right against the sidewall, under the window. The men around the fire won’t be able to see me there. Signal when it’s safe to begin.”

“What’s the signal?”

“The call of a saw-whet owl.” It was the first thing that came to his mind, simply because it was the signal that he and Red Sun Rising had agreed to use.

“What does it sound like?”

“Halfway between a whistle and a coo: *too, too, too.*”

Elijah imitated the call: “*too, too, too.*”

“That’s good.”

“How will you know it isn’t a real owl?”

“By counting. Two means ‘Danger!’ Six means ‘It’s safe. Go ahead.’”

Elijah nodded. “Two means danger. Six means safe. Can’t get those mixed up.”

“As soon as I hear six in a row, I’ll start pulling off the boards.”

Broken Trail dropped to his hands and knees. Leaving the sumac stand, he crept forward through tall grass that was wet with dew. There was good cover until he reached the bare earth of the barnyard. From that point, he was in the open. Lying on his belly, he wriggled and squirmed all the way to the chicken house. Reaching it, he lay still, the length of his body pressed along the sill timber.

Lying there, waiting for the signal, he heard the occasional burst of laughter from the few still awake around the bonfire. Closer at hand, the harmonious snores of the two men guarding the chicken coop made music to his ears.

Elijah's signal came, six sweet whistles to say that the way was clear. Broken Trail stood up. Running his hands over the boards that covered the window opening, he counted five, nailed vertically to the frame. To remove three would be enough. Maybe he could simply rip them off.

Grasping the bottom end of the first board, he pulled hard. Nothing moved. He tried each board in turn. Every nail held securely. Disappointed, he knew that since he could not pull the boards off, he would have to pry them free.

First he tried with his knife, ramming the blade tip between the first board and the frame. Too tight. He was more likely to break his knife than to free a board.

He might do better with his tomahawk. One end of its head was like a hatchet blade, the other like a curved pickaxe. If he forced the pickaxe point between the bottom end of a board and the log wall, he might be able to pry the board loose.

Facing the window, he shoved the tomahawk point under the bottom of the first board. Then he grasped the handle in both hands and pulled downward with all his strength. The nails released their hold with a rasping squeal.

A hen squawked. Over by the tree stump, the guards continued to snore.

Broken Trail set the first board on the ground, waited until the hen settled, and started on the next board. Again the nails screeched as they surrendered their grip on the wood. More hens cackled.

Inside the chicken house, Red Sun Rising must also have been startled by the noise. Did it tell him that rescue was near? Or did he think that some of his captors were breaking in, angry men too impatient to wait for morning to see him die?

"*Too, too, too,*" Broken Trail softly whistled—so softly that only Red Sun Rising could hear—hoping that he would recognize the signal.

Then he set to work again.

With three boards removed, the opening was big enough. Broken Trail returned his tomahawk to his belt, placed both forearms on the sill and hauled himself up.

By the feeble light that came through the window opening, he saw glints of gold on the chicken house floor. Then his eyes made out an elongated shape about the same size as Red Sun Rising. It squirmed, and the glints of gold moved, too.

Broken Trail pulled his shoulders higher. Leaning farther in, he saw that he would not have a clear drop from the window to the floor. Below the opening was some kind of shelf. Uncertain what it might be, he reached with one hand and grabbed . . . a handful of feathers firmly attached to a warm and startled hen. She squawked. He let go.

A nesting box! Looking to left and right, he saw that the shelf extended along the entire wall, supporting a row of nesting boxes. As his eyes adjusted to the darkness, he realized that every wall was similarly lined with shelves, and every shelf held nesting boxes. The only way to reach Red Sun Rising was by climbing through the nest of an already flustered fowl.

He paused, half in and half out of the window while the hen's clamour diminished to peevish clucking and finally to a rustling of feathers as she settled back to sleep. Silence seeped in. The only sound he heard was his own breathing. Then from out of the night came a sleepy voice.

"Hey, Levi! You hear anything?"

"Just chickens."

Broken Trail held his breath.

"More like a squeal."

"You think pigs got in the chicken house?'

"How could they? The door's locked. Anyway, it wasn't that kind of squeal."

"We'd better look."

At that instant, Broken Trail heard the call of a saw-whet owl. *Too, too.*

Plunging forward, he dived through the window opening. A wing smacked his face. An eggshell crunched under his hand. Warm slime squished between his fingers.

With a tumble and a bounce, he cleared the edge of the nesting box and landed partly on top of Red Sun Rising.

"Humph!" Red Sun Rising grunted, wrenching his body to one side.

"It's me. Lie still!"

Squawking filled the air. Ignoring the cackling, flapping chickens, Broken Trail unsheathed his knife and in a flash severed the rope that bound Red Sun Rising's wrists.

He had no time to do more. From outside the window came a man's voice. "Look at this! Somebody's pulled off half the boards."

"You think Captain Cherokee got away?"

Broken Trail rolled beneath the bottom shelf of nesting boxes, against the wall under the window.

"I can see him. He's still lying there."

"What else can you see?"

"Besides chickens, not a damn thing."

"Stick your head all the way in?"

"And get it knocked off? From the racket the chickens are making, somebody else must be inside. We better wake the other men so we can surround the hen house."

"The fellows won't be too happy with us, seein' as we didn't notice anything when we was supposed to be on guard."

"We got no choice. I'll fetch them. You stay here to keep an eye on that window."

Footsteps retreated. Peeking between two logs where the

chinking had fallen out, Broken Trail saw a man standing with his rifle aimed at the window opening. No escape that way.

When he turned his head, his eyes fell on the stone fireplace with its big chimney that reached all the way through the roof. Could they crawl up through the chimney? Well, they had to try.

Broken Trail crept from beneath the shelf. He freed Red Sun Rising's ankles and cut through the twisted kerchief that gagged his mouth.

"We're going up the chimney," Broken Trail hissed. "You first."

"Good." Flashing a quick look that was almost a smile, Red Sun Rising crawled across the dirt floor into the open fireplace. In moments his body disappeared. Broken Trail heard a scraping sound from inside. Then a muffled cry, barely audible above the cackling of the fowl.

"I'm stuck."

Broken Trail scrambled into the fireplace. Stretching up his arms, he felt two moccasined feet. With all his strength, he pulled, backing away just as Red Sun Rising landed with a thud and a shower of soot.

"My coat make me too big," he gasped.

"Take it off."

With a slash of his sharp knife, Broken Trail sent gilt buttons flying through the air. Red Sun Rising wrestled his arms from the coat sleeves and crawled into the fireplace again. Without the coat and its wide shoulder epaulettes, he had enough room to scramble up and out.

Broken Trail sheathed his knife. As he started up the chimney, the padlock on the chicken house door clicked open.

Chapter 17

FINGERS DIGGING INTO the worn cedar shingles, they lay with their bodies flat against the roof. Despite the darkness, Broken Trail could see Red Sun Rising's eyes shining with excitement. Having come so near to death, he seemed ten times more alive.

Beneath them, so close that Broken Trail could have reached down to touch them if there had been a hole in the roof, men crowded into the space between the tiers of nesting boxes. Over the chickens' clamour it was hard to hear exactly what the men were saying, especially since all seemed to be talking at the same time. But the gist was clear.

"There's his coat."

"But where's he gone?"

"Damn Cherokees set him free."

"Blood calls to blood." Broken Trail recognized Judah's deep rumble. "The hills are crawling with Cherokees. They knew we had him here."

Broken Trail nudged Red Sun Rising. "Now! Before they think to check the roof."

They wriggled over the shingles to the very edge. Here, it was only a man's height from the roof to the ground. Swinging their bodies over the edge, they dropped. They started running as soon as their feet hit the ground.

Broken Trail heard shouts and then a single rifle shot before he and Red Sun Rising reached the hillside. No one wasted another bullet. Pursuit ended within moments, as Broken Trail had expected it would. At night, no one in his right mind wanted to venture into a forest that he thought was swarming with Cherokees.

Silently Broken Trail and Red Sun Rising climbed the short distance to the sumac stand. Broken Trail plunged in first. Elijah caught him by both arms.

Seeing Elijah, Red Sun Rising stopped cold. He stared. "Who are you?"

"I'm his brother."

"Brother? I not know . . ." Not finishing the sentence, he pointed toward the crest of the hill. "Trail that way. You follow me."

Elijah was the only one whose feet made the slightest

noise as they climbed. Tripping over roots and snapping dry sticks under his boots, he stumbled after the others.

Near the top, Broken Trail glanced back over his shoulder. All he could see in the valley below were the flames of the bonfire, burning brightly again.

Red Sun Rising led them along a high trail that followed the contour of the hills. They walked for the rest of the night, and at sunrise descended into a wooded valley.

"This is far enough," Red Sun Rising said. "They not catch us."

Elijah, who looked the most in need of rest, sat down and leaned his back against the trunk of a massive oak just off the trail. Broken Trail and Red Sun Rising sat cross-legged, facing him.

Red Sun Rising peered at Elijah. "You're a redcoat. Where you come from?"

"I was taken prisoner at Kings Mountain. Moses rescued me."

"Who?"

"That's my white name," Broken Trail explained.

Red Sun Rising did not question this. He nodded. "You look like brothers." He turned to Broken Trail. "Why you not tell me you go to Kings Mountain to find him?"

"I didn't know he was there. For three years I hadn't seen him or heard any word of him."

Red Sun Rising appeared to accept this explanation. "So now you make a long trail together?"

"Yes," said Broken Trail. "I'm going home. Elijah will travel with me most of the way."

"It is good to have your brother with you on a long trail." A look of sadness spread over Red Sun Rising's face. "I travel alone."

"Back to Chickamauga?" Broken Trail asked.

Red Sun Riding sighed. "Back to Chickamauga. No scalps. No red coat. No horse." After a moment's silence, he brightened again. "It is time for the fall hunt. Winter comes soon. But in the Moon of New Leaves, we fight again." He raised his arm, flourishing an imaginary war club. "We kill the settlers who steal Cherokee land."

Broken Trail wondered how Red Sun Rising managed to keep up his resolve, for every time he was knocked down, he seemed to rise again.

"Until we reached the farm where you and I stole the horses, I thought you were already back home in Chickamauga. What happened after you left Kings Mountain?"

"That day I go to find horses. No horses where we leave them. I think Over Mountain men find them first. So I go on foot, walk many days. Then I see one fine black horse in a paddock. I think I steal that horse. Ride him home." He grimaced. "That was big mistake. Red coat very bright. White men see me." He paused. "Big, big mistake. I think I go fast to the Land without Trouble." He paused. "But then Yowa, the Great Spirit, sent you to help me."

"Reckon he did," Broken Trail answered, feeling grateful

that he had been able to repay Red Sun Rising for guiding him to Kings Mountain. He wished only that he could do more. "How far is it to Chickamauga?" he said. "If you need food for your journey, I have a little corn powder left."

Red Sun Rising shook his head. "You and your brother keep it for your long trail. I am only one day from my home." He hesitated. "It is good we meet again. You are all times my friend."

"And you are all times my friend."

Red Sun Rising rose to his feet. "If I start now, I sleep in Chickamauga tonight."

"Don't go yet," said Broken Trail. "Rest a while longer."

"When I am home, is time to rest. Tonight I see my father and my mother. For sure, they think I am dead."

"They will rejoice at your return."

"I tell everybody how I make a friend. I say he is white, but one of us."

Broken Trail stood up when he saw that Red Sun Rising was determined to leave. "Be strong," he said, and clasped his hand. "May the unseen spirits guide you."

"May Yowa watch over you and not place too many stones in your path."

"Best of luck," said Elijah, looking uncomfortable, as if he suspected that this was not exactly the right thing to say.

Red Sun Rising raised his arm in farewell, and then disappeared into the forest.

Elijah's voice broke the silence that followed. "His people

don't have a chance. The British have tried to keep the settlers in check. When the rebels take over, more and more settlers will come. They'll destroy the forest and push the Cherokees all the way to the Mississippi River. Thousands will die—people whose only crime is to live on land that somebody else wants." His voice was utterly flat, admitting no hope. "As for your friend, he'll be dead within a year."

Dead within a year. The words rang in Broken Trail's ears. In an instant, his heart felt as cold and heavy as a stone.

"At least he will die fighting."

"Is it worth it," Elijah asked, "to die in a war already lost?"

"To die with honour is always a victory."

"But does it help his people? I don't think so."

Broken Trail did not argue. He sat down beside Elijah. "Red Sun Rising asked me to go to Chickamauga with him. He wanted me to join a war party against the settlers. I wish I could help his people. But not that way."

"In the middle of a war, nobody seems able to see a better way. It's all killing, until one side or the other gives up. Then there's peace for a while, until it all starts over again. And I'll tell you what I think: the longer this goes on, the more the native people are going to lose."

"In the north," Broken Trail said, "the British are setting aside land for their Indian allies."

"Ah, but in the north the Mohawks have a chief like Joseph Brant to negotiate not only for them but for the whole Iroquois Confederacy."

"The Cherokees have Dragging Canoe."

"Dragging Canoe is shrewd and brave, but he can't read or write, and he barely speaks English. He knows nothing about the world beyond his own mountains and forests. But Joseph Brant is an educated man. He writes letters and helps to draft treaties. He has been to England and met King George. The Cherokees have no one like that to lead them, a man who is at home in both worlds."

Broken Trail did not answer. Looking down, he noticed a little patch of sunshine on the forest floor. A slender ray had penetrated the leafy canopy overhead. It reminded him of the quivering beam that had pierced the darkness of the cavity under the maple tree while he hid there after the fighting on Kings Mountain. That tiny light had been a sign, he had felt, that the Great Spirit had a plan for his life. Listening now to Elijah's words, he felt afraid of what that plan might be.

Chapter 18

FOLLOWING THE RIVER valleys in a northerly direction, Broken Trail and Elijah left behind the moss-draped trees of the south. Now birches edged the riverbanks, and the cool, crisp air was spiced with the scent of pine. Elijah thought they might be in Pennsylvania, but he was not certain.

Late in the afternoon, five days after Red Sun Rising had left them, they came upon a burned-out farm. It was a small homestead, just a couple of acres, with a swiftly flowing creek running through it. Only ashes and charred wood remained of the house and barn. When the boys poked in the ashes of the house, their prodding released the sharp smell of recent burning.

"No bodies," Elijah said. "That's good. The folks who lived here must have escaped."

"Or been carried off."

"Cherokees?"

"Too far north," said Broken Trail.

"Maybe it was neighbour against neighbour, like in the Mohawk Valley."

"Like we were burned out, back in Canajoharie." In his mind Broken Trail returned to the day that he had come home from school to find his family's home a smouldering ruin.

Elijah broke in upon his thoughts. "We should camp here tonight. There'll be trout in that creek."

Elijah was right about the trout. They caught eight, using Broken Trail's bone hooks baited with salamanders from under a log. Half they grilled on green sticks for supper; the other half Broken Trail plastered with clay to be set later in the embers to bake for their morning meal.

Night fell before they had finished eating. There was no moon. Although their small fire crackled cheerfully, darkness pressed from all around. It was good, Broken Trail thought, to have his brother with him. The closeness between them grew with every passing day.

Elijah tossed a handful of fish bones into the fire. "Did you come by here on your way to Kings Mountain?"

"No. I took the short way, over the mountains. I've never seen—"

"Hey!" Elijah broke in. "Look over there!" He pointed toward the low-growing brush at the creek bank. "Something moved. An animal."

"Likely a raccoon." Broken Trail's eyes followed Elijah's pointing finger. "No. Wrong shape."

"A wolf?"

"Too small."

The animal put a stop to their guessing. Leaving the undergrowth, it sidled toward them with its head lowered and its tail wagging.

"Well, I never!" Elijah said. "That's a hound."

The dog was brown, with a black saddle and white chest. Its paws were white, and rather large, and its tail ended in a white tip. The dog was so thin they could have counted every rib. It took a few steps toward them, setting down its paws carefully, as if testing thin ice.

"He's hungry," Broken Trail said, and he reached into the bag of hardtack. There was still some, since even Elijah avoided eating them after noticing that they were crawling with maggots. When Broken Trail held a biscuit out to the dog, it whimpered and came still closer, but not all the way.

Broken Trail reached forward until his fingers almost touched the wet, black nose. The dog stretched out its neck. Its jaws snapped as it took the biscuit. It chewed sideways, its eyes fixed on Broken Trail's face, and then sniffed about for crumbs that might have fallen to the ground.

Broken Trail offered a second hardtack, which the dog

gobbled as eagerly as the first. "You must be starving," he said, "to eat that stuff."

Sitting on its haunches, the dog looked at him expectantly, its head cocked.

"That's all you get for now."

With a sigh, the dog lay down and rested its snout on its forepaws.

All evening it watched them, warily keeping its distance but not leaving. Before falling asleep, Broken Trail wondered if it would still be there in the morning.

Sometime during the night he became drowsily aware of warm breathing against the nape of his neck and a warm furry body pressed against the small of his back.

In the morning, the dog was still there.

"Looks like we've got ourselves a dog." Broken Trail smiled as he rubbed the velvety ears.

"He won't come with us. He's waiting for his master."

"His folks aren't coming back."

"He'll wait anyway." Elijah cracked open one of the clay-baked trout that had cooked in the embers during the night.

As the dog watched, a ribbon of drool ran from its mouth, but it did not move.

"Good manners," Elijah said, "considering how he's starving."

"I'll give him another hardtack."

"Might as well give him all you have left. They'll keep him going for a couple more days."

"There are only a few." Broken Trail tossed one biscuit to the dog. "I'll save the rest to give him later."

Elijah shrugged.

When they had finished eating, Broken Trail and Elijah scattered the ashes of their fire to make sure it was dead, while the dog sat on its haunches and watched.

"Come, boy!" Broken Trail said as they started along the trail. The dog whimpered at their departure. "Come on!" he urged again.

"He can follow our scent if he decides to join us," Elijah said.

They walked about a hundred feet. The dog was still in sight. It did not move.

Broken Trail halted. He turned back. Running to the dog, he untied the canvas bag from his belt and dumped the remaining biscuits, maggots and all, under the dog's nose. He tossed the bag away.

The boys walked for a long time without talking, Broken Trail still hoping that the dog would come bounding along the path. Finally he said, "It seems an awful shame for that hound to just wait there till he starves to death. You'd think he'd have enough sense to save himself."

"Plenty of people don't," Elijah said. "So why should a dog?"

After two more days they reached the burned-out fishing village at the west end of Oneida Lake.

"I've been here before," Elijah said. "After you ran away, the long canoe stopped here on the way to Carleton Island. The village looked as if people had moved out in a hurry. There were racks for drying fish set up everywhere. Charlotte and I snooped around for signs that the Oneidas had brought you here."

"Did you find anything?"

"Your clothes. They were hidden under a log. For aught I know, they're still here. Want to look? I think I can find the log."

"Well, I don't know . . ." The idea gave Broken Trail a shivery feeling, as if they were talking about his grave. But Elijah was already walking toward the woods. Broken Trail, who could not help being curious, followed.

The log was humus now. Mixed in with shreds of wood fibre and loamy soil were a handful of buttons, a brass belt buckle, and two small boot soles, almost decomposed. Broken Trail smiled as he picked one up. "I wasn't very big, was I?"

"Size of a cricket. But you were too big for your boots even then."

"Even then? Are you saying I'm too big for my boots right now?"

"I reckon there's been some improvement, because back then, nobody could teach you anything. I remember Ma in tears when the schoolmaster said the only thing you'd accomplished all year was to carve your initials in the desk."

Broken Tail tossed the boot sole onto the ground. "I'm no good at book learning."

"You're smart enough to learn anything you want. When we were camped at Oneida Lake, I taught you to make snares the same way Okwaho taught me. You learned quicker than I did."

"It's easy to learn things that have some purpose. But I never saw the use of anything taught in school."

"Maybe someday you'll change your mind about that. Axe Carrier didn't start school until he was eighteen, when he went off to a boarding school in Connecticut, along with Joseph Brant and a couple of other Mohawks. They'd all been warriors for five years. And now they were sitting at desks in a schoolroom learning their ABC's."

"You'll never catch me doing that," said Broken Trail.

"Knowing how to read and write properly hasn't stopped Joseph Brant from being a great warrior. Why would it stop you?"

Broken Trail winced, remembering the message that the officer had written for him to carry to Kings Mountain and his embarrassment at mistaking the word "bearer" for "bear." Like it or not, reading and writing did have some use. But he wished Elijah would stop talking about school. Surely there was no place for school in the Great Spirit's plan for his life!

From amongst the shredded wood fibres on the ground Broken Trail picked up the brass belt buckle that once had been part of his clothes.

"What are you going to do with that?" asked Elijah.

"Just keep it." He slipped it into his pouch. The buckle would be a reminder of his childhood—the childhood it was his duty to forget. Carries a Quiver would disapprove. Broken Trail felt a twinge of guilt but kept the buckle anyway.

Chapter 19

SIX DAYS LATER, Broken Trail and Elijah reached the islands that marked the eastern end of Lake Ontario and the beginning of the St. Lawrence River. Across a channel half a mile wide stood a fort on a hill near the western tip of an island.

"Well, here we are," Elijah said. "That's Carleton Island, and that fort is where I enlisted in the Royal Greens nearly three years ago."

"It's a mighty big fort," Broken Trail said.

His eyes took in everything: the tall blockhouse that peeped above the ramparts, the shipyard, and the red, white and blue British flag that fluttered in the breeze. He saw the huts where native people lived outside the walls, with their birchbark canoes pulled up along the shore.

"How do we cross over?"

"We shout and jump up and down. If the sentries don't notice us, we light a fire. That brings attention. The garrison is used to people showing up here, Loyalists fleeing the Mohawk Valley."

Elijah cupped his hands around his mouth. "Halloo!" The sound rolled across the water. "Halloo!" And he waved his arms.

Broken Trail stared gloomily at the fort. He did not want to go there. If there had been any way to reach the mainland without setting foot on Carleton Island, he would have employed it. He wished that he had wings like one of those seagulls wheeling overhead. Then he would fly over the rippling water, following the river's course until he saw below him the longhouses of his village, snug within their palisade.

Elijah interrupted his thoughts. "They've seen us. Somebody's coming."

A redcoat had emerged from the fort gate and was ambling down the hill. When he reached the canoes, he hauled one to the water's edge, climbed in, and took up a paddle. The canoe rode high, skimming the little waves.

"As soon as we're across," Elijah said, "I'll clean up. Then I'll report to the officer in charge."

"I'm not going into the fort," Broken Trail said.

"Why?"

"I don't want to take any chance of seeing Ma."

"You don't have to see her if you don't want to. But it

makes no sense for you to accept me as your brother but not her as your mother."

"Maybe not. But my mind is made up. Let's not talk about it any more." Broken Trail was tired of this argument, waged not only with Elijah but also with the part of himself that suspected his brother might be right.

They stood side by side, watching as the canoe from the fort approached. Broken Trail began to feel self-conscious in his deerskin clothes, aware that he would attract curious glances and unwanted attention.

When the canoe drew up at the water's edge, the soldier looked at Elijah in his muddy coat, then at Broken Trail, and finally back at Elijah. He frowned.

"Who are you?" The question sounded like an accusation.

"Private Elijah Cobman of the Royal Greens, reporting for duty."

"Where have you been, to get your uniform in such a state?"

"Kings Mountain."

"Kings Mountain! You survived that, and then walked all the way here? Why didn't you report to Charleston headquarters?"

"Since my regiment had been wiped out, I figured it made as much sense to come back to where I'd enlisted in the first place." Broken Trail noticed the defensive tone in his brother's voice. Elijah sounded as if he knew that his explanation was not convincing.

"And him?" The soldier nodded curtly in Broken Trail's direction.

"This boy was helping the Loyalist side. He took a message from one of our armies in the field all the way to South Carolina."

The soldier looked closely at Broken Trail. "Is that the boy?" Then he spoke directly to Broken Trail, "I've heard about you. You'd better report to the blockhouse same as him."

Broken Trail resolved that he would do no such thing.

"Hop in," the soldier said.

Throughout the crossing, no one spoke.

When they had reached the other side and pulled the canoe onto the riverbank, the soldier gave Elijah a sideways glance. "No battles around here. You'll be safe." His lips curled disdainfully. Then he walked away.

Broken Trail looked after him, puzzled. "What did he mean by that?"

"He thinks I'm a coward," Elijah muttered. "To him, it looks like I came up north just to avoid the fighting. Well, he can think that if he chooses." Elijah tried to brush dried mud from his uniform with his hand. "You heard what he said, that you should report, too."

"I told you. I'm not going into the fort."

Elijah shrugged. "As you like. You don't have to take orders from him. While I'm at the blockhouse, you can look around the Indian camp for someone to take you over to the mainland. As soon as I've reported, I'll meet you back here." Without another word, he walked away up the hill and through the open gate.

He's angry, Broken Trail thought, but it could not be helped. He had the feeling that if he even entered the fort, he would somehow become entrapped, that the old life would grab him and not let him go. If that happened, he would never become a warrior or ever see his Oneida home again.

On the gentle slope below the fort stood the scattering of bark-covered huts that made up the Indian camp. They reminded Broken Trail of the temporary lodges his band had lived in after the rebels had driven them from their ancestral lands. Everything about the camp had a makeshift look. As he walked about, he saw no stretching frames set up for hides and no racks for drying fish. What did these people do, he wondered, if they did not hunt or trap or fish? What kind of life was this, to be hanging around a fort? The few people he saw standing about seemed to be doing nothing.

When he saw a warrior watching him as he wandered, Broken Trail raised his hand in greeting. He might as well, he thought, ask this man about a way to cross to the mainland. The warrior's response to Broken Trail's greeting was to stare at him with narrowed eyes. Broken Trail was familiar with that look. He knew what the warrior saw: a white boy wearing deerskins.

The warrior was a heavy-set man, not fat but well on the

way. Draped over his bare shoulders was a red blanket. His face was marked by a raised scar, the colour of a worm, that reached from the corner of his left eye to his chin. Without the scar, he would have had a sleepy face. With it, his look was menacing.

"What you want?" the warrior asked. When he spoke, his wormlike scar appeared to crawl.

"I'm looking for somebody with a canoe to take me across to Cataraqui. My home is in the Oneida village downriver from there. From Cataraqui I can walk the rest of the way."

"Oneida? You look white to me." He shrugged. "Not my business what you are. I have canoe. Tomorrow I go to trading post at Cataraqui. What you give me to carry you there?"

Broken Trail thought hard. His knife? His tomahawk? Though his tomahawk was worth more, he could manage without it. But in the forest he would be helpless without his knife.

"Well?"

"I'll give you my tomahawk."

"Show me."

Broken Trail pulled the tomahawk from his belt and gave it to the warrior. After a quick inspection, he handed it back.

"Good. Come tomorrow as soon as the sun is over the trees." He paused. "My name is Two Trees."

"They call me Broken Trail. I'll be here."

Now that his ride was settled, Broken Trail felt at loose ends. It was too soon to return to the shore to wait for Elijah. Not wanting either to linger in the Indian camp or to visit the fort, Broken Trail started walking. The path he took led northeast into the woods that covered most of Carleton Island. He had no destination in mind.

He walked very slowly. In the undergrowth small birds chirped, undisturbed by his passing. Every once in a while he stopped and gazed about. He looked down at the carpet of many-coloured leaves that covered the earth: reds, yellows and browns of every hue. He looked up through naked branches to the blue sky. A flock of geese was flying south, steadily, noisily, each bird knowing exactly where it was going.

A lonesome feeling came over him. He was about to lose Elijah. An uncertain future awaited him. He did not know his way.

What advice, he wondered, would his uncle give at such a time? Broken Trail already knew the answer. "Pray to the Great Spirit," Carries a Quiver would say. "Open your heart to the unseen spirits that are all around."

Lately, how often had he remembered to do this? Ever since he began travelling with Elijah, he had neglected even the simple obligation to give thanks after each meal.

Broken Trail stopped walking. He raised his face to the sky and reached deep inside himself for the right words, for the solemn chants and the sacred songs that his uncle had taught him. None came to him. His mind was a blank.

The only words he could think of were English words. He had gone too many days without hearing an Oneida voice. He squeezed his eyes shut and forced his mind to remember the prayers he had learned when preparing for his dream quest. And finally the words came to him, true Oneida words:

O Great Spirit, my heart is open.
I give my soul into your keeping.
Grant me your protection.

As he prayed, he felt the power of the spirits flow into him. Confidence replaced uncertainty, and the right prayer sprang to his lips:

Great Spirit, send my *oki* back to me.
Let me again see his visible form.
Let him show me a vision of my future
That I may prepare myself for what lies ahead.

He stopped and listened. A curious hush had fallen over the forest. The birds in the undergrowth had stopped chirping. There seemed to be a humming in the air, a sound that drew him toward it as if he were a fish on an invisible line. He pushed forward through the bushes.

Then he came upon the hollow.

It was shaped like a cup, and when he climbed down the side, he found warmth at the bottom, as if some of the sun's heat had been trapped. Milkweed grew there. The grey pods were papery, for they had long since burst and the silk blown away. At the bottom of the hollow was a little pool. He knelt at the edge. When he turned over a stone, a crayfish scuttled off.

As he gazed at his reflection in the pool, a faint dizziness came over him. Sweat trickled down his skin under his leather shirt. His chest felt squeezed. Gasping for breath, he pulled air into his lungs. With the air came the smell of musk—that wonderful odour he had waited so long to smell again! He heard movement behind him, a rustling. Slowly, cautiously, he turned his head.

"*Oki,*" he said softly.

The wolverine approached, head lowered, jaws open to show its yellow teeth. It spoke to him in thoughts.

"You have proved yourself worthy. Your long journey has made you a man. Now you may see the vision of your life."

Broken Trail shivered, afraid to interrupt lest his vision be lost a second time. A strange numbness filled his head. In his trance he saw a great waterfall with a rainbow shining in the mist, and he knew that this must be the waterfall at Niagara that he had heard about but never seen. The waterfall disappeared in a swirl of mist, which lifted to show a scene of armies clashing on a battlefield. In the mêlée, men in red uniforms and warriors in buckskin struggled with soldiers in blue. He saw a warrior with tomahawk upraised and knew that this was himself. The mist descended to blot out the battlefield, then lifted to reveal a town of many longhouses by a broad river. In front of one longhouse an old man sat on a log, with children clustered about his knees. And he knew that this old man was also himself.

"You will be a warrior," said the *oki*, "but you will not die in battle. You will become a great leader, both in war and in peace. When at last you go to the Land without Trouble, all nations will mourn."

The vision disappeared.

"Go now," the wolverine said. "Return to your village. It is time."

The wolverine loped away, vanished amid the milkweed stalks. Broken Trail looked about, wondering where it had gone. The strong, musky scent was the only evidence that it had been there at all.

Broken Trail climbed out of the hollow and turned back the way he had come. It was time to meet Elijah by the shore.

Chapter 20

AROUND HIM, THE little birds in the undergrowth began to chirp again. Broken Trail left behind him the pool and the hollow and the smell of wolverine, but the power of the spirits was still with him as he turned south and followed a narrow path to the river. He stood at the water's edge.

There was a splashing noise right by his feet. A bullfrog had jumped into the water. Broken Trail watched as it swam away. Then he turned west toward the fort and followed the shoreline all the way back to the spot where he was to meet Elijah.

When he did not see his brother anywhere about, he sat down near the canoes to wait. He was glad to be alone to ponder what he had seen and heard. An immense gift had been given to him, so immense that he could not grasp its meaning all at once. He was to become a great leader, both in war and in peace. That was the Great Spirit's plan for his life.

When he had prayed to see a vision of his future, he had not expected this, and yet he was not surprised. It seemed to be one of those things that he had known without knowing ever since his mission to Kings Mountain began.

Should he tell Elijah about his vision? One part of him wanted to share it with his brother; the other part advised him to wait until the path of his life became clear.

But where was Elijah? The sun was halfway down the sky. Elijah had had plenty of time to report to the officer in charge. Something must have happened to prevent him from meeting Broken Trail here, as they had planned.

Broken Trail wandered back through the Indian camp, thinking that there might have been a misunderstanding that caused his brother to look for him there. But there was no sign of Elijah.

If I want to find him, Broken Trail thought, I'll have to enter the fort after all.

With a sinking heart he headed up the hill and walked through the open gate.

There were so many buildings! Some were of wood, and some of stone. The largest was a low, sprawling structure with a wing at each end. But it was the second largest, a square, two-storey stone building, that appeared to be the most important. People kept going in and out of it. There were women of all ages, some tugging little children by the hand. There were soldiers in uniform, and old men wearing regular clothes. That building must be the blockhouse, he thought. Elijah might be there.

Broken Trail considered looking inside, and then decided against it. With its stone walls, it looked like the kind of place where he might be locked up and forced to stay forever.

Farther off was an open square where redcoats were drilling. They marched with their muskets over their shoulders. On their heads were tricorn hats like the one he had picked up on the battlefield.

Beyond the square stood row upon row of white tents. Those must be where the Loyalists lived, the white colonists whom rebels had driven from their homes.

But where was Elijah?

Over by the large, sprawling building a soldier lounged outside a door. He looked idly about, as if waiting for someone. Perhaps he would know where to find Elijah. Broken Trail walked up to him.

"Good day," he said, wanting to make a good impression, "I'm looking for Private Elijah Cobman."

The soldier lifted his eyebrows.

"Who?"

"He's a soldier who came here this morning. A canoe brought him and me across from the south shore."

"Oh, him. He's confined to barracks."

"What does that mean?"

"He can't leave barracks. He's lucky not to be in the guardhouse. Truth to tell, he's lucky not to be shot."

For a few moments Broken Trail was too shocked to utter a word. At last he blurted, "I need to see him. Where are the barracks?"

The man gestured with his thumb over his shoulder. "Right here. This is the soldiers' section. You'll find Private Cobman inside."

Broken Trail opened the door. Walking warily down a narrow hall, he peered into every room that he passed. The rooms were identical: two windows, twelve cots, and a trunk on the floor at the end of each cot. He saw no one in any of the first four rooms. The soldiers who lived in them must be the ones whom he had seen outside, marching around in the square.

In the fifth room, he found Elijah sitting on the edge of a cot, polishing a boot. He wore a clean uniform, but he did not look happy.

Chapter 21

ELIJAH WAS DABBING polish onto the leather of the boot he held in his hand when Broken Trail entered the room.

"So you found me!" Elijah said. "I thought you would, even though you had to enter the fort to look for me."

"What happened to you?" Broken Trail asked. "I waited a long time on the shore."

"I didn't get the kind of welcome I hoped for." Elijah spat on the boot, picked up a rag, and began rubbing the polish into the leather. "First, they threatened to shoot me as a deserter. Then somebody said that I must have been out of my mind, because only a madman would walk five hundred miles to Carleton Island instead of one hundred to Charleston."

"Now that you're here, do you reckon you'll be staying?" Broken Trail sat on the edge of the next cot, facing Elijah.

"If they decide that I've recovered my wits," said Elijah, "they may keep me. The garrison could use an extra man." As he rubbed, the boot took on a burnished glow. "On the other hand, they may send me back down south and attach me to another regiment. With the left wing of Cornwallis's army wiped out at Kings Mountain, the Southern Command needs reinforcements. At present, I'm confined to barracks while they make up their minds."

"Do you want to go back down south?"

"I can't say I look forward to a winter campaign in the Carolinas. Swamps full of snakes. Camps full of dysentery and yellow fever. But yes, I'm ready to go back. I'm a soldier. I'm prepared to do my duty."

Elijah set the boot on the floor, picked up its mate, and rubbed a dab of polish into the leather. "I only wish it were over. The war's lost. Another defeat, and General Cornwallis will have to see it, too. Why should more men die when it's all for naught?"

"You didn't talk like this when you were telling me about Major Ferguson picking you for his rifle company."

Elijah took a brush to the leather. "If you think that I'm afraid to die—"

"No. I would never think that."

"That soldier did, the one who paddled us across the channel." Elijah spat on the boot. He rubbed with his rag for a minute, then raised his head and looked straight at Broken Trail.

"Before Kings Mountain, I was ready to fight it out to the last, do or die."

"Like Red Sun Rising."

"Not exactly. The Cherokees have no choice. The rebels back the settlers, and the settlers won't be satisfied until every Cherokee is dead. They might as well fight till they die, because they're going to die anyway. Honour is the only thing no one can take from them.

"But it's different for the British and the Loyalists. Sooner or later, General Cornwallis will surrender. He'll hand over his sword to General Washington and everybody will go home . . . except those that are dead and those that no longer have a home." He paused. "Ever since we said goodbye to Red Sun Rising, I've been thinking about this. I no longer believe that dying for a lost cause is in any way worthwhile." He set down the second boot beside the other. "That's enough talk about me. What about you? Did you find what you were looking for?"

"What I was looking for?" For a moment Broken Trail thought that Elijah must mean his vision.

"A ride over to the mainland," Elijah prompted.

"Oh. Yes. There's a warrior going to Cataraqui first thing in the morning. He'll take me."

"I'm glad that's settled, though I'm not happy to see you go."

Suddenly Broken Trail felt very lonely. This was goodbye, and he was not ready for goodbye. He wondered when he would see Elijah again. I must tell him about my vision, he thought. There may never be another chance. Tongue-tied, he searched for English words.

"What is it?" Elijah asked. "What's wrong?"

"Nothing's wrong. Far from it. My *oki* came back."

"The wolverine? Did it show you the vision you were waiting for?"

"Yes. I saw the vision." Broken Trail took a deep breath. "It showed me many things, but explained nothing. I will become a great leader . . . my *oki* said that. A great leader, both in war and in peace. But it didn't say how. And when I die, all nations will mourn. But it didn't say why."

"All nations will mourn." Elijah was silent for a minute, apparently thinking it over. "White nations, too?"

"I'm not sure. But why not? We have an Oneida word: *Mitakuye Oyasin*. It means, 'We are all related.' It doesn't leave out anybody."

Elijah lifted his hand and laid it for a moment upon his chest, directly over the spot where the Mohawk medicine bag hung under his red coat. Broken Trail noticed the gesture.

"It doesn't surprise me," Elijah said, "to learn that you will be a great leader. I saw something of this when I was wounded and ready to die, but you wouldn't let me give up. You half-carried me for sixteen miles to a safe hiding place. While you were taking care of my wound, I sensed a power in you. It was the kind of power that helps a person to discover his own strength.

"Major Ferguson had that power, too. He inspired his troops, turned ordinary men and boys into heroes." He raised his eyes to the window, looking out as if searching for something far away. "Yes, he had that power, though in him it was mixed with faults that cost us a whole army. But we'll not speak of that, speak ill of the dead."

Elijah's eyes met Broken Trail's. "So now you're leaving. I know you're eager to be home. When you reach your village, your uncle will explain the meaning of your vision."

"He's a wise man. He'll help me to see the path that lies ahead." Broken Trail stood. "I have an idea that someday you will walk with me on that same path. It isn't every white soldier that wears a medicine bag under his uniform."

Again Elijah touched his fingers to the place where the medicine bag lay. "Who knows? I'd like to go on another long trail with you. But whatever happens, remember that we're brothers, whatever else we may be." He paused. "What was that word, again?"

"*Mitakuye Oyasin.*"

"I won't forget." Elijah stood up. He grabbed Broken Trail and gave him a hug. Broken Trail gulped hard to force down the lump in his throat as he turned toward the door.

Darkness fell quickly. A cold wind was blowing from the west when Broken Trail reached the shore. He crawled under a canoe for shelter. He probably could have found a more comfortable place to sleep, he thought, but he did not want to take any chance of Two Trees leaving without him in the morning. When the sun rose above the trees, he wanted to be ready.

Chapter 22

IT WAS A COLD MORNING, with spirals of white mist rising from the dark water. Broken Trail stood shivering by the shore. He was stamping his feet to shake the cold out of them when he saw Two Trees approach from the Indian camp.

"So you come. Give me tomahawk. Then we leave." The wormlike scar down the side of his face wriggled as he spoke.

Broken Trail pulled his tomahawk from his belt and surrendered it to Two Trees. This was not a good bargain. But what choice did he have, in his eagerness to reach home?

Two Trees handed him a paddle. They eased the canoe

into the water. Broken Trail knelt in the bow, glad to have the warming exercise of paddling.

After rounding Carleton Island's western tip, they entered the channel that lay between Carleton Island and Wolfe Island, its larger neighbour. This was where Lake Ontario ended and the St. Lawrence River began. By the time they passed the eastern end of Wolfe Island, the mist had lifted. To the north, on the mainland, Broken Trail saw a slim column of smoke rise above the trees.

"Cataraqui?" Broken Trail called over his shoulder.

"Yes. Smoke come from trader's lodge."

As they drew nearer, the ruins of a fort came into view. Within the tumbled walls, he saw the bark-covered lodge from which the smoke was rising. Although he had never been to Cataraqui before, he knew that this must be the lodge of the fur trader, Louis Tremblay, son of a Huron mother and a *coureur de bois* father, to whom hunters and trappers of many nations brought furs to exchange for rifles, axes, blankets, beads and other goods. Broken Trail would have liked to return home with a present for Catches the Rainbow. He could imagine her smiles at receiving a brooch with coloured glass stones or a necklace of shiny beads. But he had nothing to trade for such a treasure.

When the canoe reached shore, Broken Trail stepped into the shallow water and pulled up the bow. He had no desire for a parting conversation with Two Trees, nor had the Mohawk any words to spare for him. After the briefest of farewells, each went his separate way, Two Trees to the trading post and Broken Trail along the path that would take him home.

On his left were granite cliffs and tree-clad hills where only a few withered leaves still clung to the branches. On his right, off shore, were many islands, some large and wooded, but others little more than a rock boasting a single gnarled tree. He scarcely glanced either to the left or to the right, for his mind was filled with thoughts of home.

Carries a Quiver would rejoice to see him alive and to learn about his vision. Catches the Rainbow would smile in her quiet way and comment on the sad state of his moccasins. His friend Young Bear would listen to his story and be happy for him that his *oki* had appeared, and then they would make plans to hunt deer together, as they had done many times before. Most important of all, he was ready to prove his readiness to be a warrior.

That evening, after lighting a small fire and preparing a bed of spruce boughs, he ate the last of the sweetened corn powder. As he ate, he thought of the two warriors who had given it to him. He would never know who they were. But they had been the first persons whom he met on his long trail. When he finished eating, he remembered to strike the ground with his right fist and give his thanks to the Great Spirit.

His thoughts turned to Elijah. Many evenings on their journey together they had sat and talked beside a campfire like this one. Looking into the flames, Broken Trail summoned up the image of his brother in his mud-smeared red coat, the coat that concealed a Mohawk medicine bag hanging from a thong around his neck.

To Broken Trail, this medicine bag was the token of a special bond that was beyond the natural bond of brotherhood. The unseen spirits that watched over Broken Trail also protected Elijah, although he was not a native either by birth or by adoption. The more Broken Trail thought about this, the more he came to feel that the Great Spirit's plan for him included his brother. Why else had the Great Spirit sent him to Kings Mountain to find him?

As the flames died, the image of Elijah faded. Broken Trail lay down on his spruce-bough bed. He was cold, having no blanket to wrap around him. But tomorrow night would be different, for he would be sleeping on a warm, cushiony bearskin in the longhouse, with family and friends nearby.

The following morning, having nothing left to eat, he set out hungry. He could have caught a fish, for the St. Lawrence teemed with many kinds, but his greatest hunger was the hunger to be home.

He walked all day. As his shadow stretched longer and longer in front of him, he walked faster and faster. And then in the golden light of early evening, he saw a blur of smoke above the trees. A little after that, the palisade of pointed poles came into view, and above the palisade, the roofs of the three longhouses, one for each of the Oneida clans: Wolf, Turtle and Bear.

At the entry to the palisade he paused. His heart beat quickly, and he was breathing heavily. He must compose himself, he thought. It was important to look confident, as if there were nothing unusual in taking two moons to accomplish what should have been achieved in ten days. Squaring his shoulders, he strode forward, neither fast nor slow, keeping his eyes straight ahead.

The first persons to notice him were two small boys walking side by side across the empty dancing circle. They glanced at him, halted, and then looked at one another. No smiles. If anything, they looked alarmed. That did not matter, he told himself. He did not care whether children welcomed him, or not.

More important were the three warriors he now noticed strolling toward the longhouses. These were men of high standing in council: Hunting Hawk, Black Elk and Swift Fox. They were his uncle's friends, although not of his clan.

Broken Trail walked up to them and raised his hand in greeting.

"I have returned," he said, as naturally as possible. "My *oki* has appeared to me, and I have seen a vision of my life."

They stopped walking. Swift Fox was the first to raise his hand in greeting. The others followed, lifting their arms slowly and with hesitation.

Turning to the two small boys, who had moved closer in their curiosity to see what was happening, Swift Fox commanded, "Go to the Bear longhouse. Find Carries a Quiver. Tell him that his nephew has returned."

The boys raced away to deliver their message.

Swift Fox turned to Broken Trail. "No one expected to see you again."

When Broken Trail entered the longhouse, it looked the same as when he had left it two moons ago. Warriors lounged about, talking. Little girls, busy with their beadwork, sat on the edges of the sleeping platforms with their legs dangling over the side. On one platform five young boys huddled in a circle, intent on a game of dice. One tossed the dice in a flat-bottomed bowl, and all leaned forward to see how they had landed.

In a row down the centre of the longhouse, between the sleeping platforms, the six cooking fires burned brightly. Broken Trail looked for Catches the Rainbow at the third fire, and there she was, standing with a long-handled ladle in her hand while she chatted with the woman whose family slept on the opposite platform and shared the same fire.

Catches the Rainbow, too, looked the same as the last time he had seen her. A woman of medium height, she had a broad, pleasant face more accustomed to smile than to frown.

A moment passed before anyone noticed him. And then it seemed that all eyes turned at once, as when one deer in a grazing herd spots danger and all lift their heads. Broken Trail heard a collective gasp. Wide-eyed children drew closer to their mothers. No one smiled. For a moment there was silence, and then a murmur rose, sounding alarmingly like a low growl. Many who had been his friends looked at him as if he were a stranger.

At her first glimpse of Broken Trail, Catches the Rainbow's eyes held shock. Then her expression changed with lightning speed. A glow spread across her face as if suddenly, as her name implied, she had caught a rainbow.

At the fourth fire, a slim youth wearing a bear-claw necklace jumped up. When his eyes met Broken Trail's, he raised his arm in salute. Skirting seated family groups and treading carefully to avoid tripping over bowls, pots and babies, he made his way to Broken Trail.

"Young Bear greets his friend," he said firmly. As they clasped hands, Broken Trail's spirits rose. He did not care how many people scowled, so long as Young Bear welcomed him home.

Catches the Rainbow filled Broken Trail's bowl with meat and broth and gave him a piece of cornbread for dipping. Now this was real food!

As people finished eating, they drifted to the space around Catches the Rainbow's cooking fire. By the time the women had cleared away the pots and dishes, every member of the clan's twelve families had gathered to hear Broken Trail's story.

While he was speaking, most people listened quietly, but from time to time frowns and grunts signalled disapproval. Warriors shook their heads at his decision to act as a messenger for the British. His rescue of Elijah drew a mixed reaction, as he expected it would. To save a brother was praiseworthy; but why, three years after the Oneidas had adopted him, did he still regard that white soldier as his brother?

After listening to his story, families returned to their own places in the longhouse. Children were the first to climb onto the sleeping platforms to settle for the night. The women followed, leaving the men still talking by the sinking fires. From overheard snatches of conversation, Broken Trail knew the talk was all about him.

Finally, he and his uncle were the only ones still talking by a fire.

"In council, there will be much discussion," Carries a Quiver said. "Warriors of all three clans will deliberate what to do about you."

"You mean, am I fit to be a warrior?"

"That is the question."

"Why should there be any doubt? My *oki* appeared. I received a vision that foretold my future. And I've just explained why I was away so long."

Carries a Quiver raised his hand in a gesture to end the discussion. "Leave all to me. As your teacher, I am the one who will speak for you in council. Tomorrow, you and I shall talk more about this. Tonight, you need to sleep. From the dark circles around your eyes, I think you have had little rest for many days."

Broken Trail glanced at the sleeping platform where Catches the Rainbow was already deep in slumber.

"Yes, tomorrow will be soon enough."

As he lay down on his thick bearskin, he listened to the wind rattling the elm-bark roof slabs overhead. It was good to be inside, where the air smelled comfortably of smoke, food, and the sweat of many people crowded together. After so many cold lonely nights and long hungry days on the trail, he fell deeply asleep.

Chapter 23

THE NEXT MORNING Broken Trail sat facing his uncle on the ground outside the Bear Clan longhouse. Carries a Quiver was a man of fifty winters, Catches the Rainbow's older brother. His eyes were deep set, with creases at the corners. His face was worn, dark and broad. In one hand he held a bone chipping tool, and in the other a half-formed arrowhead. He appeared to be studying the arrowhead, but Broken Trail knew that his uncle's mind was really on him.

"When you disappeared, some people thought you had returned to your white family," Carries a Quiver said. "They believed that your heart had remained with them all along."

Broken Trail looked down, feeling guilty to have deceived

his uncle, for he knew how much truth there was in this.

Carries a Quiver continued: “Others said that you ran away in shame because the Great Spirit denied you a vision, knowing you unfit to be a warrior.” He hesitated. “That was not the worst thing people said.”

“What could be worse?”

“They feared that you had turned into a wendigo.”

“No!” Broken Trail looked up, horrified. He had been prepared for some to reject him on his return. But for anyone to think he had turned into a wendigo was beyond his worst imagining. Wendigos were fierce and evil. Part man and part devil, they lurked in the forest to seize and eat little children. The only way to kill a wendigo was to burn its heart. If people thought he had turned into a wendigo, they had every reason to be afraid. And so did he.

“Uncle, what did you think?”

“I thought you were dead.”

Lowering his eyes to the arrowhead, Carries a Quiver pressed the chipping tool to the hard flint. A flake flew off, landing on Broken Trail’s knee. He did not move to brush it off.

Carries a Quiver continued. “Because I was the one who had prepared you for your spirit quest, I was sure you were ready. But perhaps there was still more to be done.”

“That must be so. When my *oki* appeared the second time, it said, ‘You have proved yourself worthy. Your long journey has made you a man.’ Then it allowed me to see the vision of my life.”

"From what you told us last night, I see that a good life lies before you. But no life is without trouble. You may face more than most men because of who you are. From the start, there were warriors who said you would someday betray us."

"That's the sort of thing Walks Crooked would say."

"His has always been the strongest voice among your enemies."

"I don't know why he hates me so much."

"As your skills increase, his enmity grows. He can't bear to see a white boy surpass his son. You hunt better than Spotted Dog, swim better, and follow a trail better. But Walks Crooked has resented you right from the beginning. When you came to us as a child, he advised us to kill you. He says we should never adopt white prisoners. 'Kill them all,' he says."

"My Cherokee friend Red Sun Rising hates settlers, but he is still my friend."

"Walks Crooked's hatred is deeper than that of any man I have ever known. It goes back to his first battle, when he was your age." Carries a Quiver set down the chipping tool and arrowhead. "At that time, he had a different name. It was in the days when the Six Nations of the Haudenosaunee stood united in the Great Peace. We were allies of the English in their war against the French."

"I know," Broken Trail said. "Our enemies, the Hurons, helped the French."

Carries a Quiver nodded. "The French had a fort at

Niagara. The English asked our help to capture it. Walks Crooked was in that battle. A musket ball struck his leg just above the ankle. He fell to the ground. The French drove back the English. When the English saw that they could not capture the fort, they retreated, taking their wounded with them. Walks Crooked called out to them, but they did not help him. They left him to die. Somehow he escaped. It took him four days to crawl on his belly back to our camp. By then it was too late to set the bone properly to make his leg straight again. That is why one foot points sideways while the other points straight ahead. Ever since, he has hated white people."

"For that reason he is my enemy." Broken Trail sighed. "Maybe he will never change his mind. But if the warriors will take me on the next war party, I will show what I can do."

"That is the best way. Prove your worth. Then none will listen to those who speak against you. It takes patience." Carries a Quiver held up the arrowhead to inspect the point. Their talk, it appeared, was finished.

"Uncle, I shall keep these words in my heart." Broken Trail rose to his feet. "If I may, I would like to find Young Bear. This will be a good day for hunting."

Carries a Quiver smiled. "I wish you luck on the hunt. We are short of food for the winter. If you shoot a deer on your first day back, your welcome will be certain."

"That was a fine adventure you told us about last night." Young Bear slung his quiver over his shoulder. "You must be proud that your *oki* is a wolverine. They're fierce fighters."

Side by side they left the longhouse. Broken Trail's heart felt light. After his long absence, he was at last doing what he loved most, setting off on a hunt with his friend. This was the best time of year for hunting, the brief season of mild days between the Moon of Falling Leaves and the arrival of the first snow.

"Did you ever lose hope," Young Bear asked as they walked along, "when you had to wait so long for the rest of your vision?"

"There were times when I feared that my *oki* had forgotten about me or that I had offended the Great Spirit. It was a trial to have to wait so long. But I never lost all hope."

"Waiting is the hardest part. The nine days that I fasted and prayed were the longest in my life. They dragged on and on. But when my vision came, it was as sudden as a thunderclap. I heard a terrible scream. When I looked up, I saw an osprey fly down from the sun with a lightning bolt in its talons. Its speed was like an arrow's. I trembled with fear."

Just imagining the sight made Broken Trail shiver. He stopped walking and turned toward Young Bear. "Then what happened?"

"The osprey spoke from above, circling the spot where I stood. 'Young Bear,' it said, 'Do not fear. I am your *oki*. Until the day appointed for your death, you will be safe in the shadow of my wings.' When it had finished speaking, it circled upwards, making wider and wider circles until it vanished in the clear sky."

Broken Trail breathed hard as he pictured the power and beauty of the magnificent bird. “And then?”

“I fell to the ground and remained in a trance while unseen spirits showed me the vision of my future. I saw how I would die in battle, pierced with many arrows. Then I woke.”

“You told me part of this before I set off on my own spirit quest. I knew that you would die in battle. You told me you had your death song ready, in case your first war party should be your last. But you never told me how your *oki* came to you.”

“At first it was too powerful to talk about. And then you were gone. I never even told all the details to the council of warriors. I still haven’t told anyone except you. I’m not sure I ever will.”

They walked on. Their way took them through fields where women were harvesting the last of the crops. Pumpkins, squash and gourds of many shapes made bright splashes of colour—orange, green, yellow and gold—against the dun earth of the planting mounds.

“My uncle says that we are short of food for the winter,” Broken Trail said.

“That is so. Our storehouses are half empty. As you know, we reached our new lands too late to clear more than a few fields for planting. A hungry winter lies ahead. If you shoot a deer, your mother will be proud.”

“I would like to deserve her praise. She is a good mother. I fear that I have shamed her. I think the other women pity her to have a son like me.”

"When you bring back a deer, she'll be proud again."

Leaving the fields behind, they followed a path that curved and wound ahead of them into dense forest. Broken Trail noticed a scrap of antler velvet dangling from an overhanging branch twice his height above the ground. A big elk, he thought, for its antlers to have reached so high when it rubbed them clean.

They walked in single file, Young Bear leading. As the wilderness closed around them, they were careful not to make a sound. A word, a cough, or the snap of a branch cracked underfoot could spoil the hunt.

Suddenly Young Bear halted. He stood for a moment, his right hand uplifted. Then he lowered it, looked over his shoulder and pointed to Broken Trail's bow.

They stood at the edge of a glade where the tall grasses of summer now lay flattened and yellow. Except for one alder that wore a bittersweet vine like a necklace of orange beads over its crooked branches, the surrounding bushes were bare. Behind the alder, something moved. Something much bigger than a deer. It moved again, and now Broken Trail saw the grey-brown of the animal's flanks. Wapiti. An elk. It raised its head with a slow, deliberate motion, displaying the widest rack of antlers that he had ever seen. Turned slightly away from the boys, the elk did not see them.

Broken Trail held his breath. Young Bear motioned him to go ahead.

He's giving the kill to me, Broken Trail thought with a rush of gratitude. And he prayed that his arrow would fly true.

In a gliding crouch, keeping windward of the elk, Broken Trail edged closer. The animal was still out of range. Unsuspecting, it lowered its head to continue grazing. He came nearer. A few more paces and he was close enough. He reached with one hand for an arrow from the quiver on his back, fitted the arrow to the string, raised the bow, and slowly pulled the arrow back. From this angle it would pierce the elk's great, beating heart. One eye shut, he stared along the length of the shaft, then let it fly.

"Good! Good!" Young Bear cried out. Silence did not matter now. With a loud grunt, the elk crashed through the trees, snapping branches as it staggered away. Young Bear caught up to Broken Trail and slapped him on the shoulder. No need to hurry. From the snorting and thrashing in the brush ahead, they knew that the elk was down and dying.

When they came upon it, the last shudder was passing from its huge body. Blood lay spattered on the ground and on the broken bushes that the elk had crushed. Joy filled Broken Trail's heart, and he saw the same gladness on Young Bear's face.

Young Bear stood back while Broken Trail spoke to the elk.

"Brother, pardon me for killing you. My people need meat, and I need to earn their good opinion. When your ghost reaches the Land without Trouble, tell the Great Spirit that this is why you died."

Broken Trail skinned the elk, which was the duty of the

one who made the kill. Then Young Bear helped him to strip off the meat in sheets. They took the heart and liver from the carcass and hacked off the antlers. Finally they pulled the two upper canine teeth so that each of their mothers could have a beautiful elk's tooth pendant. Little more than bones were left for the foxes and crows to share.

With everything heaped upon the green hide, they had a heavy load. Laughing and sweating, they dragged it like a sled. When they reached the village, they hauled it to the longhouse of the Bear Clan, for that was their clan and so the meat was for them.

Catches the Rainbow was smiling and laughing among the women while they set up racks for smoking the elk meat. Every bit would be saved for winter. Standing proudly apart, Broken Trail watched the women work.

Carries a Quiver stood beside him. "The council of warriors will take note of this. Tomorrow I shall speak to them about accepting you as a warrior."

His words made Broken Trail glow with pride. Soon he would have a scalp lock like Young Bear's, to which he would fasten trophy feathers as soon as he had earned them.

That night, before the families had settled on their sleeping platforms in the longhouse, Broken Trail gave one of the elk teeth to Catches the Rainbow, and she gave him a new pair of moccasins and a set of arm muffs for cold weather.

"I made these while you were away," she said, "because in my heart I knew you would return."

The next morning Broken Trail rose early and walked down to the river. It was a blustery day. The wind, blowing from the west, rippled the water and drove ragged clouds across the sky. In the middle of the river a bateau was ploughing its way upstream. It had a mast with a crossbar intended for a square sail, but the mast was empty. He counted twelve men working the oars. The boat was low in the water. It must be on its way from Montreal to Carleton Island, he thought, loaded with winter supplies. Tomorrow it would reach its destination, the landing place below the fort. In an odd way, he felt that the boat's passage brought him nearer to Elijah. A secret link.

He was still watching the bateau creep by when suddenly he sensed that someone had come up beside him. He heard no footsteps. Turning his head, he saw Walks Crooked at his shoulder. How could a man with a twisted foot approach so silently?

Walks Crooked was a lean, sinewy man. He had piercing eyes and a weasel-like face that was made particularly ferocious by four vertical scars on his left cheek, a memento of the cougar whose claws had raked his skin. No one doubted his courage. A man with a crippled foot could have lived his life without shame as a medicine man or a canoe maker. Instead, he had overcome his handicap to become the fiercest of all the warriors, famous for his ruthlessness. The sorrow of his life was not his maimed foot but the failure of his lazy son Spotted Dog to achieve prowess in anything.

"A war party is planned, a raid against the Mississaugas. Perhaps Broken Trail wishes to be part of it?" There was a taunt in his voice. "There is talk of admitting you to the society of warriors, though some say that you are the sort who runs away when fortune turns against him."

Broken Trail's heart filled with anger. "*Some say!*" Who would have been the first to spread such a lie about him? None other than the man standing at his shoulder, a sneer on his face.

Broken Trail stiffened his features, not letting his fury show. He was suspicious of Walks Crooked's motives in inviting him along, but what could he do about it? He had long dreamed of the day when he would be old enough to go on the warpath with the men of his band. Now his chance had come.

"Take me with the war party," he said coldly. "Let me prove what I can do."

Chapter 24

BROKEN TRAIL RAN his fingers through his scalp lock. It was too soft, too fine. The hair did not stand up in a stiff crest the way it should. It wasn't even the right colour. But at least he looked more like a warrior than before, when his hair had hung nearly to his shoulders, like a boy's. His naked scalp, which still stung from having every excess hair pulled out, had been rubbed with bear grease until it shone.

The war party would leave at dawn the next day. Eight warriors and four youths would take part. The youths were Broken Trail, Young Bear, Spotted Dog and a slightly older boy named Red Crow.

Broken Trail was ready. Carries a Quiver had given him a

new tomahawk. Catches the Rainbow had made him a scalp-lock decoration using elk hair and beads. There was only thing that his scalp lock lacked, and that was a trophy feather. Two trophy feathers would be better. Or three.

Carries a Quiver painted Broken Trail's face in the colours of war, one side black and the other red. He painted with great care to make the pigments smooth. As he worked, he was very quiet. The look on his face was of a man preoccupied with disturbing thoughts. Broken Trail did not pry. He supposed that his uncle was concerned about him, setting forth on his first war party.

Tonight there would be a feast and dancing. By the time Carries a Quiver finished applying Broken Trail's war paint, savoury odours were rising from the cooking pots. As the women set out the food, dogs began to swarm, at first skulking at a safe distance, and then sneaking closer to the fire. Four younger boys with clubs stood guard to keep the dogs from approaching the food.

One year ago it had been Broken Trail's task to keep the dogs away, for these boys were not much younger than he. Until today, he had looked like them. But now he had a scalp lock and face paint like a warrior's. Although he knew the boys, he did not speak to them as he took his place among the men. Young Bear sat on one side of him and Red Crow on the other. This was Red Crow's second war party. For Broken Trail, Young Bear and Spotted Dog, it was their first.

The women brought them dishes heaped with meat and boiled water lily bulbs. Broken Trail was too excited to feel hungry. But he ate everything, just to show that he had a man's appetite. He could hardly wait for the feasting to be over and for the dishes and pots to be cleared away.

At the first warning thumps on the drums, his pulse quickened. He watched while the dancing circle was cleared and fresh wood heaped upon the fire. Then the twelve members of the war party rose from their places. Broken Trail and Young Bear stood up at the same moment. For an instant Broken Trail's eyes locked on Young Bear's, and he saw his own excitement reflected there. This was it. Their first war dance. Silently the dancers stationed themselves in the dark shadows beyond the firelight. Swift Fox, who would lead the dance as well as the war party, carried a spear dressed with bright streamers.

DUM, doom, DUM, doom. War drums began to beat, deep-voiced and strident. The shaking of rattles joined the thumping of the drums. Then the singers began to chant, clacking together the polished sticks they held in their hands. Broken Trail's heart pounded to the beat. Bouncing on his toes, he sensed the rhythm all through his body, faster and faster, until he felt he would explode if he had to wait much longer.

Swift Fox sprang first into the dance circle, brandishing his spear, its streamers flying. After him came Black Elk, then another, and then it was Broken Trail's turn. With a leap and a yell he joined the dance, lifting his knees high, stamping his feet and fighting with shadow enemies. He held high his new tomahawk and, with the flat side of its head, struck the war post as he danced by. This was what he had dreamed of for so long—to be part of the dance.

Flames swept into the sky. DUM, doom, DUM, doom. Faster and faster the drums beat and the rattles shook and the singers chanted, their clacking sticks adding to the din.

Whooping and leaping, Broken Trail danced in a frenzy. The warrior ahead of him shouted out his history of brave deeds and boasted about the Mississauga scalps he would take. Broken Trail had no past exploits to brag about. But what he lacked in experience he made up for in imagination. Brandishing his tomahawk, he mimed the havoc he would wreak. With wild yells, he smote the war post every time he circled by, and with every blow a phantom enemy fell. By his twentieth circling, twenty foes lay dead.

And then it was over. Swift Fox led the dancers, one after another, out of the circle of light. The chanting, the stick clacking and the rattling stopped. The drums fell silent.

Broken Trail sank exhausted in his place by the fire, completely out of breath. Young Bear, his brow beaded with sweat, leaned toward him. "I wore out my moccasins in that dance."

"So did I. And they were new this morning."

"We're real warriors now."

As the fire died to embers, people straggled back to the

longhouses. On his family's sleeping platform, Broken Trail unrolled his bearskin and lay down, the beat of the drums still throbbing in his head.

In the morning, Carries a Quiver touched up his war paint, adding a red ring around his right eye—the side of his face that was painted black—and a black ring around the other.

"This will help you to see far," he said. "You must watch out for enemies."

His face wore the same worried expression that Broken Trail had noticed the day before.

"Do not worry about me. I shall return safely, and with honour."

"How can I not worry about you? I thought you were dead, and now that you have been restored to us, you are setting out to face danger again."

"Uncle, you agreed that I should go on the next war party. You told me, 'Prove your worth.'"

"Those were my words. Yet I fear that this war party is a mistake."

"A mistake? Why do you think that?"

"In my opinion, it would be better to stay home and use the time for hunting. I said this in council, but those in favour of a war party argued that a raid on the Mississaugas was the fastest way to obtain food for winter. The final decision was not mine." He sighed. "I should not be talking to you like this, not now. You must not go into battle with thoughts that weaken your resolve." He laid his hand on Broken Trail's arm. "Be strong. Keep your eyes about you. Don't rely on your *oki* to keep you safe if you walk upwind of your foe."

Broken Trail laughed, "No enemy will smell fear upon me."

"You have never been in battle."

Swift Fox led the line that jogged westward along the trail. Behind him came Walks Crooked, his lurching gait not slowing him. Spotted Dog, right behind his father, puffed and panted to keep up. Broken Trail was fourth, and then came the rest, with Black Elk at the end.

Half the warriors were armed with rifles; the others had brought their bows, preferring the silence of the arrow to the speed of the bullet. Among the boys, only Spotted Dog owned a rifle, a fine one given to him by his father to celebrate the success of his spirit quest.

The beat of the drums still throbbing in Broken Trail's head drove out most of his troubling thoughts. He set aside his uncle's concerns. For a long time he had wanted to go on a war party. Nothing could spoil it now.

The raid had been carefully planned. A four-day journey westward would bring the war party to the Mississaugas' main village, which stood beside a river that ran south into Lake Ontario. The Mississaugas were a forest-dwelling people, hunters and gatherers. They did not cultivate great fields of corn, beans and squash as the Haudenosaunee did. Their storehouses held dried meat, fish, berries, nuts, maple sugar and wild rice.

While one group of Oneida warriors took baskets of food from the storehouses, another group would steal all the Mississaugas' canoes. They would load six canoes with food and set the rest set loose to drift downriver. Two to a canoe, the Oneida raiders would paddle the loaded canoes downstream to Lake Ontario, then they would turn east. When they reached the St. Lawrence River, the current would bear them swiftly home.

The warriors jogged on and on. They squelched through bogs where tiny channels of water flowed sluggishly between clumps of bulrushes. Broken Trail's moccasins were soon caked with the mud of swamps. The war party pushed its way through the undergrowth of lowlands that smelled sour with decaying vegetation.

They did not stop to hunt or fish, for they had brought along a good supply of pemmican packed into leather bags. A mixture of dried meat pounded into flakes and then mixed with fat and dried berries, this was food that gave strength, tasted good and would last for a long time.

As they sat around the campfire each night on the trail, the warriors talked about battles they had fought, dangers they had faced and enemies they had slain. Like the other boys, Broken Trail listened and dreamed about the day when he would have his own exploits to brag about. Yet he began to have a feeling, and the feeling grew, that this war party would not bring honour to those who took part.

Here they were, planning to steal food that the Mississaugas had stored up for winter, so that the Mississaugas would go hungry instead of them. What they were doing, he thought, was not much better than what General Sullivan's army had done to the Oneidas when it destroyed their crops and burned their homes.

This was not the kind of thought he could share with any other member of the war party, not even Young Bear. Aside from Carries a Quiver, the only person that might understand was Elijah, and Elijah was far away.

On the third day, when the sun stood directly overhead, Swift Fox called a halt.

"We have entered the Mississauga hunting grounds," he said. "The war party will now separate into four groups, each with its own assignment. The four groups will return to this spot tomorrow to share what each has learned."

The warriors sat in a circle on the ground. Swift Fox looked around, meeting the eyes of each of the others in turn. "Black Elk, Walks Crooked, Hunting Hawk and I will each choose one youth and one experienced warrior. My group will search out all the trails that lead to the Mississauga town. We must decide upon the best route, as well as locate paths for escape in case we are discovered."

Choose me! Choose me! Broken Trail pleaded silently. He was good at reading trails, and eager to earn Swift Fox's respect.

Swift Fox continued. "Black Elk's group will locate the storehouses and find out how they are guarded.

"Hunting Hawk's group will learn where sentries are posted and what signals they use to communicate.

"Walks Crooked's group will find out how to steal the Mississaugas' canoes and also select the best place to load them."

Swift Fox chose first, passing over Broken Trail to choose Red Crow.

Broken Trail did not allow his disappointment to show. It didn't matter greatly, he told himself. He would willingly serve under Black Elk or Hunting Hawk. Anyone but Walks Crooked.

Walks Crooked won't choose me, he assured himself. He'll want Spotted Dog so he can keep an eye on him and cover up his mistakes.

Black Elk chose Young Bear.

Now it was Walks Crooked's turn. Broken Trail kept his head down. Help me, *oki*, he silently pleaded. Make him say Spotted Dog!

Walks Crooked announced his choice. "I'll take Broken Trail."

So Hunting Hawk was left with Spotted Dog, that clumsy lump whom his own father would not choose. Good luck to him! If Spotted Dog snapped even one dry branch under his foot, all their lives would be in peril.

But why, Broken Trail wondered, had Walks Crooked chosen him?

Chapter 25

BROKEN TRAIL HAD faced danger more than once before now. For the most part, he had faced it unafraid. But now he was afraid. What he feared were not the bullets and arrows of the Mississaugas so much as a silent knife in his back.

It was some comfort to have Smoke Eater as part of his group. Although not friendly to Broken Trail, he was not hostile, either. But he was blind in one eye. Broken Trail would feel a little safer if Smoke Eater had two good eyes, and much safer if Walks Crooked were not his enemy.

Starting out deep in Mississauga territory, Walks Crooked, Smoke Eater and Broken Trail made their way toward the river. They crept through heavy brush, avoiding trails, crawling under bushes rather than pushing through them. Once they saw a party of Mississauga hunters glide by, silent as wolves on the prowl, and lay still until the hunters had passed. The sun was halfway down the sky when Broken Trail and his two companions reached the riverbank.

Walks Crooked, standing at the base of a tall spruce tree, motioned Broken Trail to stand beside him.

"You see this tree?"

How could he not see it? It was right in front of them, stretching up and up into the sky. Broken Trail nodded.

"You may wonder why I chose you," Walks Crooked said. Before Broken Trail could think of a reply, he continued, "I wanted you because you're small and light. You can climb higher than someone heavier, and be better hidden in the branches."

Broken Trail, who had never before seen any advantage in being small for his age, nodded his head and hoped that this was Walks Crooked's true reason.

"Climb up to the top. From there you will be able to see not only the canoes, but everything up and down the river." He paused. "Your task is to count the canoes and see if are they guarded."

Broken Trail nodded.

"And judge the speed of the current."

"I can do that."

"And look downstream to see whether there are any fallen trees, big rocks or sandbars that would block canoes from floating away. Finally, I want you to look for a good spot where we can load the canoes."

"I'll find out everything."

All this would be important information, Broken Trail realized. Excited by the challenge, he swung himself onto the spruce's lowest branch. Quickly he scrambled up the trunk.

The drooping branches with their dense needles soon hid the two on the ground from his sight. As Broken Trail climbed higher and higher, bark blisters burst under his hands and resin stung his scratched skin. When he reached the crown, clinging like a bear cub to the trunk, he saw hills and forest stretching to the horizon. Below him was the river, and across the river was the Mississauga town.

The town had no defences on the riverbank. But on the land side there was a palisade of tall, pointed poles. It curved in a half circle, embracing the town, with each end of the palisade extending right into the river. At the rear of the town, a gap in the palisade gave access to the forest.

Inside the palisade, the whole life of the town lay spread before him. Women were scraping hides on stretching frames. Meat slabs and whole fish hung on drying lines. A man was applying hot pitch to the seams of a birchbark canoe. Children and dogs were chasing each other around the dome-shaped lodges.

The homes were different from those in an Oneida town. The Mississaugas were not longhouse people, where a clan's many families lived under the same roof. In the Mississauga town it looked as if each family had its own house, a bark-covered lodge with a hole at the top for smoke to escape.

Broken Trail noticed that several lodges had no smoke

hole. A couple of these were very small, not high enough for a man to stand upright inside. They looked exactly like Oneida sweat lodges, and that was likely what they were. But others were much larger. Those must be the storehouses, he thought, crammed full with the food that the war party planned to carry off.

Looking down on the scene, Broken Trail felt no hostility to the Mississauga people. They were not traditional enemies of the Haudenosaunee, as the Hurons had been. Because the Mississauga hunting grounds lay north of the Oneidas' ancestral lands, there had been little contact between the two nations before the Oneidas were driven from their old territory. Since then, a few skirmishes had taken place. Nothing approaching outright war. From now on, Broken Trail thought sadly, the Oneidas and the Mississaugas would be enemies. This war party would make certain of that.

Broken Trail felt a voice of protest within him struggling to be heard. What was he doing here? He knew the answer. He was here because he had to prove himself. He had no choice about that. This war party was his first big test. He must not fail.

On the riverbank lay the canoes. He counted twenty-three, tied together at the bow in bunches of three or four. They were unguarded. That was fortunate, for he had expected to see somebody keeping an eye on the canoes, either a boy or an old man.

He turned his attention to the river. Looking upstream,

he watched for some floating object that would reveal the speed of the current. At length a broken branch, still sporting a few brown leaves, drifted past. His eyes followed it downstream until it fetched up, below the town, against a fallen willow tree that half blocked the river. Debris was piled up in the lee of the willow. This was the sort of obstacle that concerned Walks Crooked. If the canoes were cut free, that fallen tree would stop many, perhaps most, from drifting downstream.

Now that he had all the information he had been asked for, Broken Trail climbed down. Walks Crooked and Smoke Eater were waiting for him.

They listened in silence to his report, nodding from time to time. Neither interrupted until Broken Trail described thc fallen willow that half blocked the river.

"How far is that willow from the town?" Walks Crooked asked.

"The distance of an arrow's flight."

"Too close! It means we cannot push the canoes into the river and trust the current to carry them far enough downstream. If we do, the fallen willow will certainly trap some, and then, if the Mississaugas take alarm, they can round them up and come after us."

"But the tree can help us," Broken Trail said. "The riverbank beside the willow will be a good place to load the food." He rubbed his hands on his leggings, trying to wipe off the sticky spruce resin. "First, we push all the canoes into the river. When the canoes float by the willow tree, we can have warriors waiting there to snag the first six, then shove off the rest around the end of the tree."

"A fine plan," Smoke Eater looked at Broken Trail approvingly. "It's good to have a loading place that even a man with one eye can find in the dark."

Walks Crooked grunted. It sounded as if he agreed but did not want to admit it. Broken Trail suppressed a smile. He was beginning to feel that he had Smoke Eater on his side.

Chapter 26

THE NEXT MORNING the members of the war party met. They sat in a circle, with the leader of each group ready to report.

Swift Fox began. Using a sharpened stick, he drew a diagram in the earth, showing the position of the river and the town. Then he traced several trails leading north, south and west from the opening in the palisade. He marked a spot upriver from the town.

"Here is a sandbar where we can cross the river in order to reach the town through the forest." His stick moved rapidly over one of the trails he had already marked. "And this trail is the one we follow. It is the most direct."

Hunting Hawk reported next. He said, "At night, only two warriors are on guard, positioned separately near the opening in the palisade. No one guards the canoes. There is no sign that the Mississaugas expect an attack."

"What about the storehouses?" Swift Fox asked.

"I can answer that," said Black Elk. "There are seven storehouses, grouped together close to the palisade on the downstream side. They are unguarded. One way to reach them is by tunnelling under the palisade. Another is to remove four or five poles in order to make a gap wide enough to pass storage baskets through. Either way is possible, providing that Hunting Hawk's group has first taken care of the guards near the palisade opening."

"But where do we take those storage baskets?" Swift Fox turned to Walks Crooked. "What have you learned about the canoes?"

After reporting everything that Broken Trail had found out, Walks Crooked added, "I'll wait with Smoke Eater by the fallen willow tree downstream while Broken Trail frees the canoes and shoves them into the river. As the canoes float by, Smoke Eater and I will catch the first six and push all the others around the end of the tree for the current to carry away."

"Twenty-three canoes? It won't be easy for one person to deal with that many, especially an untested boy."

Without waiting to be asked, Broken Trail called out, "That's not too many. I've seen how they are tied. It won't be hard."

Swift Fox turned to Walks Crooked. "How will Broken Trail reach the canoes without being seen? Even after the guards have been removed from the palisade opening, it will be too risky for him to try to sneak all the way through the village to reach the riverbank. There'll be almost a full moon tonight."

"He won't go through the town," said Walks Crooked. "It's quite simple. Smoke Eater and I will fasten him under a floating log with a reed to breathe through. He will swim underwater across the river. His arms will be free to control the log. It will seem to drift ashore."

Broken Trail gasped. Walks Crooked had not told him about this part of his plan. To swim underwater concealed by a floating log was part of every boy's training for war. He had practised it in the summer. But at this time of year the very thought made him shiver. What if he lost consciousness in the frigid water? What if he drowned? For an instant he thought that this might be a scheme to kill him. But no. Walks Crooked would not risk the success of the raid just to rid himself of Broken Trail. He must think that Broken Trail really could do it.

Swift Fox shook his head. "It is an excellent trick. But the water will be too cold."

Walks Crooked smiled unpleasantly. "Broken Trail brags that he is a true Oneida. If he is, then his blood will not freeze. Smoke Eater and I will take him a short distance upstream. When he is under the log and under the water, the Mississaugas cannot see him."

Swift Fox looked unconvinced. "This close to winter, I would not ask anyone to do it."

Broken Trail seized his chance. "My body is hard. I can do it."

Swift Fox looked intently at him, as if to make certain that he really meant it and was not just trying to placate Walks Crooked.

"Very well," he said. "If you are sure."

Broken Trail noticed that he looked impressed.

Walks Crooked, Smoke Eater and Broken Trail set out first. Before the raid could begin, they had to hew a suitable log and carry it to the riverbank. The other warriors would wait until later to cross even farther upstream at the sandbar.

The sun had set but the moon had not yet risen. There was little chance that any hunters or food gatherers would be in the forest this late. But Walks Crooked was taking no chances. He had sent Broken Trail high in the spruce tree again as their lookout while he and Smoke Eater cut down a basswood tree.

They were far enough east of the river that the chop, chop of their tomahawks would not carry as far as the Mississauga village on the west bank.

Sitting astride a branch and clinging to the trunk, Broken Trail felt numb from holding one position too long. He moved his shoulders and wriggled his toes in an effort to keep his blood moving and to ward off the chill. Part of him was eager to begin his assignment. The other part worried about the challenge that lay ahead, half wishing that he had declined it when he had the chance. The water would be brutally cold. Maybe his bravado had been a mistake. It had been easy to say, "My body is hard. I can do it." But what if he couldn't?

The moon had risen by the time Walks Crooked and Smoke Eater had the log ready. Broken Trail shinnied down the tree and helped them carry it to the river. The log's length was slightly greater than Broken Trail's height, and its diameter about the same as the thickness of his body. Basswood, being soft, had been easy to cut; being light, it was easy to carry.

They set down the log on the riverbank. Across the river, there was no sign of activity in the Mississauga town. Broken Trail looked at the cold, dark water in front of him—the water that he would have to plunge into to reach the other side.

"Take off everything except your belt and breechcloth," Smoke Eater said. "Keep your knife. I'll look after your clothing and your tomahawk and give them back to you at the willow tree."

Broken Trail pulled off his shirt and untied the laces that attached his leggings to his belt. Finally he took off his moccasins. He braced himself, trying not to shiver as he followed the others into the river.

Walks Crooked and Smoke Eater guided the log until the water was deep enough for it to float easily. Broken Trail ducked below the surface and positioned himself on his back under the log, with one end of his breathing reed in his mouth and the other sticking straight up above the water.

He felt Smoke Eater's hands fasten the strap under the back of his neck to support him at one end of the log, and Walks Crooked's hands attach the strap to hold his feet at the other. Then he felt the thrust as they pushed the log out into the river.

As long as he kept the clear end of the reed above the surface, he could breathe. Stroking steadily with his arms, he knew that he was moving well. The water began to feel not quite so cold. Either the exertion was warming him, or his chilled flesh was already numb. He just had to keep moving and keep breathing.

This wasn't going to kill him, he told himself. The only thing to worry about was the swiftness of the current, for if there had been a mistake in judging that, he might go ashore at the wrong place.

It seemed a long time before he felt stones scrape his buttocks. First he freed his feet, and then his neck. Still clinging to the log, he lifted his head and took a deep breath. Blinking the water from his eyes, he saw that the calculation of the current had been correct. At the water's edge in front of him were the canoes.

He manoeuvred the log out of the water and lay behind it. With the night air blowing on his wet skin, he felt colder than ever. Naked except for his sodden breechcloth, he could not help shivering.

Pulling his knife from its sheath, he crawled to the nearest bunch of canoes and set to work, hacking and sawing at the fibrous ropes that linked them. His numb fingers could scarcely grip the knife. His awkward position, lying on his stomach, made the work harder still. But he dared not allow any part of his body to be higher than the canoes.

There were six ropes. When he had cut them all, Broken Trail returned his knife to its sheath. Crawling on hands and knees, he placed a pair of paddles in the first canoe and dragged it into the water, not releasing it until he felt the tug of the current that would carry it away. Then he went back for the next. One after another, he set the canoes loose. Gentle bumping and splashing were the only sounds he made. He kept working until he had launched more than half.

Nothing stirred in the Mississauga village. In the distance, wolves howled. Closer by, a great horned owl called. *Hoot. Hoot. Hoot.* Another owl answered from farther off.

Then suddenly the air erupted with a savage whoop, wavering and pulsing, high and wild. This was not the Oneida war cry. Something had gone wrong.

He threw himself flat on the ground behind a canoe. Men were shouting. People were running in every direction. But there was nowhere for him to run. At his back was the river; in front, the Mississauga town.

Rifles cracked. Arrows whizzed in flocks, some with metal arrowheads that glinted in the moonlight. They flew in both directions: toward and away from the fallen willow. In an instant, he realized that he could not go to the willow tree; his own comrades would shoot at anyone running to them in the dark. And if they didn't kill him, the Mississaugas would. Broken Trail did not have the strength to swim across the river again. He was trapped.

His only safety lay in the forest beyond the Mississauga town. To reach it, he must go around the end of the palisade. With a shudder, he waded back into the icy water and splashed upstream, away from the willow tree and the fight.

After clearing the end of the palisade, he stumbled onto the bank. Then he turned west, toward the forest. War whoops rang in his ears. Numb and shaking with cold, he ran clumsily, tripped and fell, banging both kneecaps on hard rock. He rose to his feet, staggered, and then fell again. After his second fall, he lacked the strength to rise.

Still within earshot of the battle cries, he crawled through scratchy undergrowth to the nearest thicket and lay exhausted in the matted grass. I can still defend myself, he thought. I have my knife. I'll stay here until there's enough light to see where I'm going.

The eastern sky faded from black to grey. From the direction of the willow tree came war cries and battle sounds. That was where he should be, fighting at the side of his comrades. He felt like a coward to be hiding while the battle raged.

Chapter 27

BROKEN TRAIL LAY ON his side with his knees pulled up, trying to curl his shivering body into a ball. This was no night to spend in the open, wearing nothing but a breechcloth. Snowflakes drifted into the thicket, melting when they touched his bare skin.

Gradually the sounds of battle ceased and the bushes around him emerged from a dark blur to distinct shapes. The first birds began to stir. A crow cawed. A cardinal whistled: *purdy, purdy, purdy, purdy*. He heard the cheerful voice of a chickadee.

But there was another sound as well that reached his ears, a low moan that rose and ebbed. Not the call of a bird. Not an animal noise, though at first he thought it might be. The long, drawn-out "Ooooohhh! Ooooohhhh!" was human. Not a woman. Not a child. The groans were deep and hoarse. It sounded like a man in great pain. But surely no warrior, no matter how badly injured, would allow himself to moan like that.

Say something, he silently urged. Speak Oneida or speak Mississauga. Let me know what you are.

If he were a Mississauga, wounded in the fighting, Broken Trail would take his clothes. Clothing was his first need if he was not to perish from the cold. He also needed a weapon. A warrior would carry a war club or a tomahawk. Maybe a gun.

But what if the groans came from a fellow Oneida, a member of the war party? Then Broken Trail would help him any way he could.

On his hands and knees he crept toward the sound. A thin skin of soil and dry grass barely covered the hard limestone. Separating Broken Trail from the person who lay moaning was a long fissure in the rock, twice the width of a man's foot. Though it was too narrow to fall into, it would still be a hazard for anyone walking there in the dark.

He crawled carefully across the fissure, not wanting to send pebbles clattering down its sides. He was good at this. No other boy in his village could creep so stealthily up to a grouse and snatch it from the nest.

Just a bit closer. Now he saw a man lying on the ground,

or at least he saw a man-size horizontal lump the colour of buckskin. He saw a rifle too. For safety, he must gain possession of that gun before doing anything else.

Holding his breath, he wriggled forward until he was close enough to grab the rifle. Just as he snatched it away, the owner's head turned. And Broken Trail found himself looking into Spotted Dog's terrified eyes.

"Broken Trail?" Spotted Dog mumbled, sounding as if he could not believe it. His eyes looked a little less terrified—but only a little. He hated Broken Trail. Now Broken Trail had him at his mercy. They both knew it.

"What happened to you?" Broken Trail asked.

"I think my leg is broken. I stepped into that crack in the rock."

Broken Trail sat back on his haunches and stared at Spotted Dog. His war paint was smeared, and his left leg lay bent at an angle that was not natural. This was a fellow Oneida. Whatever Broken Trail thought of him personally, nothing could change that fact, or the duty that he owed.

Spotted Dog rubbed his eyes with the back of his hand and snivelled, "I can't walk."

"Let me see." Setting the gun well out of reach, he ran his fingers over Spotted Dog's legging. A little below the left knee there was a sharp point beneath the skin. "You're right. It is broken."

Spotted Dog whimpered, "Help me!"

Broken Trail felt like asking: What would *you* do if our

situations were reversed? For a fleeting moment he was tempted to taunt Spotted Dog with this question. But why torture him when he was already in pain?

"I'll help you." He thought for a moment about what needed to be done. "Do you have some strong cord in your pouch?"

"I have sinew cord."

"Give it to me. Your tomahawk, too."

Spotted Dog pulled the tomahawk from his belt. It was steel-headed and new—worth many beaver pelts. Taking it in his hand, Broken Trail liked the heft of it, the feel of the smooth wood and the sharpness of the blade. Walks Crooked always gave his son the best of everything.

Broken Trail laid the tomahawk on the ground and undid the laces that held up Spotted Dog's left legging. After pulling it off, he untied the laces of the right legging.

"You don't have to take off both my leggings," Spotted Dog whined. "Only one leg is broken."

"As you can see, I'm almost naked. If you want my help, you must share your clothes. Keep your shirt. I'll take the leggings. I need moccasins too."

"I have an extra pair in my pouch."

"Give them to me."

Spotted Dog pulled them out and handed them to Broken Trail. They were new buckskin moccasins, and only a little too large.

As soon as he had put on the leggings and moccasins,

Broken Trail felt better. The leggings were twice as wide as they needed to be, and too long. Although there was nothing he could do to make them narrow enough for his skinny legs, he could adjust the length by shortening the laces that attached them to his belt.

After doing this, he looked around. Close by grew a gnarled old cedar tree, its roots gripping cracks in the rock. At its base, a low-growing juniper spread its twisted branches. A juniper clump made a good place to hide; he knew that from experience.

Broken Trail pointed toward the tree. "You'll be safer over there than lying out in the open. I'll pull you to it." He grabbed Spotted Dog under both armpits, ignoring his grunts of protest and pain, and dragged him to the base of the tree. Then he went back to pick up the tomahawk and rifle. He gave the rifle to Spotted Dog.

"Keep this for now. I'll use your tomahawk to cut splints to set your leg. While I'm away, don't make a sound."

"Will you return?"

"If I weren't coming back, wouldn't I take your rifle, too?" Leaving Spotted Dog to think this over, he slipped away into the woods. He moved warily as he searched for what he needed, for there was great danger this close to the Mississauga village.

It was full daylight by the time he returned, carrying two strong, straight sticks and an armful of moss. Spotted Dog was lying just as Broken Trail had left him.

"Now I'm going to set your leg," Broken Trail said. "You have to reach back and hold tight to the tree trunk. Get ready. I need to pull hard."

Broken Trail braced his feet. He knew he had to bring the two ends together in a perfect meeting. He also knew that if he failed to do it right, Spotted Dog would walk crooked, like his father, for the rest of his life.

Spotted Dog, lying on his back, reached both arms above his head and took a firm grip on the tree trunk. "I'm ready."

Broken Trail grasped Spotted Dog's left foot with both hands and pulled as hard as he could.

Spotted Dog went limp. He had fainted.

At the sudden lack of resistance, Broken Trail fell backwards. He lay still for a few moments, then propped himself on his elbows. His first attempt to bring the two ends of the bone into line had failed. What should he try next? He looked at the unconscious boy; then he looked at the tough, old cedar tree, with its roots so tenaciously gripping the rock. It gave him an idea.

Broken Trail picked himself up. He bent over Spotted Dog and unlaced his belt. Using the belt as a tie, he bound Spotted Dog's wrists together behind the tree trunk. Now it didn't matter whether Spotted Dog was conscious or not. In fact, it was better this way, for his muscles were slack and would not clench.

Broken Trail took hold of Spotted Dog's left foot and pulled steadily until he felt something give. With some adjusting, he brought the ends of the bones into line and then tied the moss and sticks firmly in place.

The leg was set. Broken Trail had watched warriors do this before. He looked upon his work with satisfaction, knowing that he had done a good job.

Spotted Dog's eyelids flickered. His eyes blinked open. For a moment he looked confused. Then, in an instant, he realized that his hands were tied behind the tree trunk. His lower lip trembled. "I see now that Broken Trail plans to kill me."

"I wouldn't have bothered setting your leg if that was what I planned to do."

He untied the belt. When he had freed Spotted Dog's hands, he helped him to put his belt and breechcloth back on. But not his pouch. Broken Trail needed that; he fastened it to his own belt.

Spotted Dog pulled himself to a sitting position and leaned against the tree trunk. His broken leg, sticking out in front with its packing of brown moss, looked somewhat like a small log. "My first war party," he said bitterly.

"Mine, too," Broken Trail answered. "Were you in the battle by the willow tree?"

"No. Were you?"

"I couldn't get to it. I was trapped on the riverbank. Where were you?"

"With Hunting Hawk," he sniffled. "We were creeping up on a sentry when a dry branch snapped underfoot."

Broken Trail wanted to say: Under whose foot? But he knew the answer. It would not have been Hunting Hawk's misstep that alerted the enemy.

"The sentry leapt like a cougar. Hunting Hawk's knife missed its mark, and so he was the one who died. The sentry gave a war whoop."

"I heard it. The whole Mississauga village heard it."

"Then he scalped Hunting Hawk."

"What were you doing? Couldn't you have killed him while he was taking the scalp? With a tomahawk like this one?" He picked up the shiny, deadly weapon.

Spotted Dog turned his head away.

"I see." So Spotted Dog had run away. Well, hadn't he done the same? This first war party had been a disaster for both of them. He sat down beside Spotted Dog, beginning to sympathize.

"Here's what I think. You can't walk. You're too heavy to carry, and I can't drag you all the way home." He paused. "There's no chance of stealing a canoe, not after last night. I must leave you here and go for help."

"Where will you find help? In this country we have no friends."

"Back to our village."

"And leave me alone?"

Broken Trail pretended not to notice the tears that spilled down Spotted Dog's cheeks, making an even worse mess of his war paint.

"Is there food in your pouch?"

"Pemmican."

Broken Trail opened the pouch. From a leather bag he took out a chunk of pemmican the size of a man's fist. He cut off two pieces, each no larger than a walnut.

"We'll eat this now. You keep the rest." Broken Trail took a bite. Until he started chewing, he had not realized how hungry he was. It was good, although not as good as the pemmican Catches the Rainbow made. Spotted Dog's mother should have used more dried cranberries and less grease.

"It took our war party four days to get here," he said between bites. "If I hurry, I think I can return home in three." He plucked a handful of dry grass to wipe his fingers. "Then there'll be another day or two for rescuers to reach here by canoe. So this pemmican must last you for about five days."

"Five days!"

"Can you think of a better plan?"

When Spotted Dog failed to answer, Broken Trail said, "I'll start out now. You can keep your knife and tomahawk. I'll take your rifle."

"Don't take my rifle."

"I'll need it to hunt for food . . . unless you want me to take the pemmican."

"But then I'd starve!"

Broken Trail's small stock of sympathy drained away. He stopped himself from saying, "You're lucky I don't leave you for the Mississaugas to scalp." What he did say was, "Afterwards, I'll give you back your rifle."

Broken Trail rose to his feet. "You'll be as safe right here as anywhere. Lie still under the juniper. Your clothing is the same colour as the needles lying on the ground. With the tree at your back, nothing can come up behind you."

"A cougar could leap from the branches."

"You'll have the tomahawk and your knife."

"What good will they do me against a cougar? If you leave me, I shall sing my death song this very day."

Broken Trail spoke sharply. "Do that if you like. The Mississaugas will be searching the forest. If somebody hears you, you'll die soon enough." He paused. "But if you want to live to be a man, lie low, be silent and wait." He handed the tomahawk to Spotted Dog. "Summon your *oki*. It will protect you."

Spotted Dog's knuckles were white where he gripped the handle of the tomahawk. His voice trembled. "I have no *oki*."

"No *oki*?" Broken Trail did not know what to say. "But . . . but you told everyone about the golden eagle that—"

"I lied." He turned his face away. "There was no golden eagle. I couldn't let my father know that my quest had failed. He would die of shame to have a son who was fit only to dig garbage pits."

Broken Trail took a deep breath and let it out slowly. "Walks Crooked held a great feast to celebrate your vision. He gave you this rifle . . . "

So it was all a lie. There was no protector to watch over Spotted Dog while he waited in the forest. No wonder he was afraid.

He'll wish he hadn't told me, Broken Trail thought. If I walked in his moccasins, I don't think I'd want to live.

Chapter 28

BROKEN TRAIL FORDED the river at the sandbar upstream from the Mississauga town. He was on an unfamiliar path—not the one that the war party had taken. But he knew which way was east, and that was the direction he had to go. He ran at an easy pace that would carry him forward without exhausting his strength.

The exercise kept him warm, even though he was naked from the waist up. He kept moving all day. At dusk he stopped beside a creek. It was the time when animals came to drink—a perfect opportunity to try out Spotted Dog's fine rifle.

He waited behind a tree, ready to shoot the first thing

that came along. A hare was what it happened to be. Broken Trail had never before hunted with a rifle. But he had a clear shot, and the hare was barely half an arrow's flight from where he stood. Staring down the rifle's barrel, he pulled the trigger.

The shot rang in his ear. The rifle butt punched his shoulder, knocking him onto his backside while the hare bounded away.

The clear shot turned out to be a clear miss.

Shamefaced, he glanced to either side, as if there might have been a witness to his failure. But only the little birds, their twittering silenced by the noise, had seen. Broken Trail looked down reproachfully at the gun, his expectations greatly disappointed.

With a sigh, he looked for a fish hook in Spotted Dog's pouch, but did not find one. What was he to eat? This close to winter, frogs were already hibernating, deep in mud. Crayfish? He turned over a stone in the creek's shallow water and lunged for the scuttling creature that tried to flee.

Darkness fell. As he sat beside his campfire, picking shreds of flesh from a stack of crayfish claws, unevenly roasted, he thought about his brother. The hare would not have escaped if the rifle had been in Elijah's hands. Elijah was a sharpshooter. One of the best. Hand-picked to serve in Major Ferguson's rifle company. But now the fight had gone out of him. He saw no point in dying for a lost cause.

Or for a bad cause?

If Elijah were here now, Broken Trail would explain how

important it was for him to prove himself as a warrior, and how he had struggled to suppress his doubts about the war party. Even his uncle had felt that the raid upon the Mississaugas was a mistake, although how great a mistake no one could have foreseen.

It was cold that night. Next morning the ground was white with hoarfrost, and tiny icicles like pointed teeth hung along the overhang of the creek bank where water had sprayed.

Broken Trail crept shivering from the pile of leaves where he had slept, and he set off again. Around midday he came to a river and turned south to follow it downstream, knowing that all watercourses in this region flowed into Lake Ontario. As he jogged along, he passed a dead campfire, recent because the smell lingered. Who had camped here? Mississauga warriors? White traders? The ashes offered no clue.

By sundown the river had begun to widen, telling him that he was near its mouth. Not far ahead, downstream, he saw a single tendril of smoke rise above the trees. Was this smoke from the fire of the same travellers whose campsite he had seen earlier in the day? He needed to know. If they were Mississaugas, he must be very careful that they did not see him. But if they were white traders, he might ask for their help.

Leaving the path, Broken Trail moved silently through the forest. When he reached the spot from where the smoke was rising, he peered through the bushes.

Two white men sat by a fire, roasting bannock on sticks. Their canoe lay overturned on the riverbank. The men wore fringed buckskin shirts and leather leggings. Both had untrimmed beards and long hair that straggled from beneath their broad hats. Although one's beard was brown and the other's streaked with grey, they looked enough alike to be brothers.

Traders, he thought. If there were fur bales under that overturned canoe, then those men must be headed for Montreal. If so, they would pass right by his village.

With Spotted Dog's rifle over his shoulder, Broken Trail strolled into the campsite. When the men saw him, they had their hands on their guns before he could blink an eye.

"Friends, I'm glad to see you," he announced, "because I need help."

The younger man gaped.

The older one laughed. "What kind of a boy are you?"

"I'm Oneida, though born white."

The man laughed again. "Son, you ain't fish nor fowl nor good red herring. But how d'you reckon we can help you?"

"I was on a long trail with a friend. Two days ago he broke his leg. I left him hurt bad. I need help to bring him out."

"Where'd this happen?"

"Upriver."

"We ain't going back upriver to help nobody. Under that canoe we got eight bales of beaver pelts. We're taking 'em to Montreal, and we're mighty eager to get there."

"I'm not asking you to go upriver. Just take me with you

as far as the Oneida village east of Cataraqui. It's not out of your way."

The younger man pulled his bannock from the stick and chewed it slowly. His eyes were on the older man. "What d'you think, Abel?"

"I think we might . . . if he makes it worth our while."

"What do you want from me?" Broken Trail asked.

"We'll settle for that rifle," the man called Abel said.

"It isn't mine to give away. It belongs to my friend."

"The same friend that's lying in the bush with his leg broke?" Abel snorted. "I reckon he'd give his rifle to save his life."

Broken Trail hesitated. He had promised Spotted Dog that he would return the rifle. But the time saved might mean the difference between life and death.

"It's a bargain."

"Are you sure we got room for him?" the younger man said.

"We can squeeze him in with the pelts." He turned to Broken Trail. "Sit down. If you're going to join us, we might as well feed you. I'm Abel. My brother here is Seth."

"My name is Broken Trail."

Seth handed him a hot bannock, still on the stick. After he had eaten it, Abel gave him a filthy blanket. Rolled in the blanket close to the fire, Broken Trail drifted off while the brothers were still talking. Later, waking briefly, he heard snores from the other side of the fire and fell asleep again.

In the morning Abel and Seth loaded the fur bales into the canoe, making a space for Broken Trail to squeeze in. Sitting with his arms wrapped around his knees, he could barely move. But he was warm.

Soon the canoe reached the river mouth and entered the choppy, open water of Lake Ontario. Heavy with cargo, it rode so low that every wave threatened to swamp it. Spray soaked Broken Trail's face and hair and wet the fur bales piled around him.

Paddling became easier as soon as the canoe reached the islands where Lake Ontario flowed into the St. Lawrence River. Seth and Abel turned the canoe northeast in order to follow the channel that lay between Wolfe Island and the mainland, that being the shorter way. Broken Trail recognized the western tip of Carleton Island, before Wolfe Island hid it from his view, and he had a glimpse of the flag that flew over Fort Haldimand. Maybe Elijah was still there, a member of the garrison. Or had he been assigned to a different regiment and sent back to the Carolinas? Someday Broken Trail would have to search for him all over again.

Once past Cataraqui, the canoe, helped by the current, moved swiftly along the St. Lawrence River. Soon Broken Trail would be home.

What awaited him there? How many of the twelve who had set off on the war party were still alive? Maybe he and Spotted Dog were the only ones who survived. His thoughts turned to Young Bear, who at the age of thirteen had his death song ready in case his first battle turned out to be his last. Broken Trail prayed that Young Bear had not been killed in the fighting, though he knew that it was now too late for prayer to help.

Darkness had fallen when Seth and Abel dropped him off at the Oneida village. Broken Trail handed the rifle to Abel, who cradled it appreciatively in his arms.

"Good luck, little Indian," said Abel.

"I hope you reach your friend in time," Seth added.

Stiff from sitting cramped so long, Broken Trail walked on wobbly legs through the opening in the palisade.

He hesitated before entering the Bear Clan longhouse, dreading what he was about to learn. But there was no time to spare. He lifted the corner of the hide covering that hung over the entry and stepped inside.

It was almost a surprise to see that everything looked so normal, with each of the six cooking fires burning in its proper place. And yet an unaccustomed stillness hung in the air. He heard no laughter, no chatter of conversation. This was a house of mourning. He saw grief on every face.

At the third fire pit, Catches the Rainbow was stirring something in a big pot. Maybe she felt him watching her, because she raised her head and looked directly at him. Her mouth opened, but he could not catch what she said. Everyone turned and stared at him.

Carries a Quiver rose from his spot beside the fire and approached, his arm upraised in greeting. His features did not move, but Broken Trail saw joy in his eyes.

"Ho! Broken Trail lives and has returned," said Carries a Quiver.

"A couple of fur traders brought me back."

A silent crowd gathered. And there was Young Bear in their midst, looking unharmed. Broken Trail's heart lifted, but this was not the time to show his gladness.

"Walks Crooked told us how you swam the river to cut the ropes of the Mississauga canoes," Carries a Quiver said. "He told us that arrows and bullets flew like a blizzard. He was certain you had been killed."

"The shooting came from two directions. I was caught in the middle, unable to reach the place where we planned to meet." Broken Trail looked around, searching for other members of the war party. "Who else came back?"

"Black Elk and Young Bear arrived first. They came in a canoe loaded with baskets of rice. They had set out before the Mississauga sentry raised the alarm, and paddled all night. In the morning they stopped to wait for the others to join them. When none did, they realized that their canoe was the only one that had escaped.

"Today Swift Fox, Walks Crooked and Smoke Eater returned. They found one of the canoes that you had set loose to float down the river. According to them, the Mississaugas took no prisoners. Apart from you and these five, all the rest of the war party are dead. A terrible price to pay for a few baskets of rice."

"One more survived," Broken Trail said. "Spotted Dog is alive . . . or was when I left him."

"You left him?"

"His leg was broken, and he's too big for me to drag or carry. I set his leg, then left him hiding not far from the Mississauga village. I came as fast as I could to bring help."

"Did he have any food?"

"Pemmican. It may be gone by now."

Carries a Quiver turned to a boy who stood near by. "Go to the other longhouses. Get Walks Crooked, Swift Fox and Black Elk. Tell them that Broken Trail has returned and that Spotted Dog lies hurt in the forest. Broken Trail will lead a rescue party to him. There is no time to lose. It must leave tonight." He turned to Broken Trail. "You should eat something while the others prepare for the journey."

Broken Trail took his place at Catches the Rainbow's fire. She brought him baked squash and stewed rabbit. As she watched him eat, her dark eyes shone with joy.

After gulping down the food, he climbed onto his family's storage platform, a wide shelf over the sleeping platform, where he quickly found a pair of his own leggings, a buckskin shirt and tall winter moccasins. By the time he had dressed, the canoes were ready.

Broken Trail paddled in the bow of Swift Fox's canoe. Walks Crooked and Black Elk were in the other. All night they fought the current and a west wind. As the sky changed from black to grey, they passed the mouth of the river that had borne Broken Trail south in Seth and Abel's canoe. Just after sunrise, they reached the outlet of the next river. There they stopped and pulled up their canoes onto the sandy shore.

"Where are we?" Broken Trail asked.

"Just downstream from the Mississauga village," Black Elk answered. He stretched to ease his muscles. "After we have eaten, we'll paddle upriver as close to the village as we dare and hide the canoes downstream from the willow tree."

Swift Fox lifted a food basket from his canoe. He took out the pemmican bag and cut off a chunk of pemmican for each person. All except Walks Crooked sat down to eat, relaxing against the canoes. Walks Crooked took no food. He paced back and forth, his twisted foot leaving prints at an odd angle to those of his other foot. He did not look as if he wanted to speak with anyone.

While Broken Trail ate, he watched a raft of merganser ducks. They floated with their bodies so closely packed together that it appeared a person could walk across their backs and not fall through. When the ducks moved off in their compact formation, it looked as though they were being towed away.

Once or twice Walks Crooked threw a glance in Broken Trail's direction. His face was a frozen mask. Only his restless pacing betrayed the turmoil of his feelings. He looked afraid that his son would not be found alive.

Chapter 29

BROKEN TRAIL HAD HIS mouth full of pemmican when Walks Crooked stopped pacing. He stood in front of Broken Trail and stared at him. Feeling anxious under the scrutiny, he chewed harder, hoping that somehow this might ward off whatever questions Walks Crooked was thinking of asking.

Walks Crooked spoke abruptly. "Was my son in good spirits when you left him?"

Broken Trail kept chewing while he thought how to answer. He could not mention Spotted Dog's unmanly tears and certainly not his shameful confession. When he could put off answering no longer, he swallowed the thoroughly chewed-up pemmican.

"Spotted Dog was ready to meet death."

Walks Crooked looked satisfied. "A warrior must always be prepared for death. But my son's *oki* will protect him. A golden eagle is noble and strong."

Broken Trail said no more.

Now Swift Fox called the others together. He took a stick and drew a line in the sand. "This line is the river." He drew a half circle beside it to represent the palisade and the dwellings it enclosed. "This is the Mississauga town." Then he jabbed at a point downstream from the town. "Here is where we'll hide the canoes. Black Elk will wait there to guard them.

"As you know, I have searched out all the trails in the region of the Mississauga town." He hesitated. In the moment of silence, Broken Trail knew that Swift Fox was remembering the two who had searched those trails with him—both killed in the battle at the willow tree. Swift Fox continued. "When we have made our detour around the town, Broken Trail will lead us to Spotted Dog. When we find him, we shall carry him to the canoes and be on our way."

They pushed the canoes into the water and took up their paddles. There was little traffic on the river this late in the fall. Most traders had already transported their cargos of furs to Montreal. Only once did they meet a freight canoe travelling south. Sitting in comfort in the centre, a white man smoked his pipe while eight warriors paddled. The paddlers in the freight canoe scowled ferociously at the

Oneidas, whose bristling scalp locks identified them as foes.

"Mississaugas," Swift Fox said. "It is fortunate for us that they are working for the trader. We four would have little chance against eight of them."

The sun was directly overhead when they went ashore. After dragging the canoes into a willow thicket on the riverbank, they left them for Black Elk to cover with brush.

Swift Fox led them west and then north on a narrow path. They moved as silently as smoke through the trees. Chickadees, hopping among the branches, called cheerily to each other and paid no attention. If there had been a Mississauga sentry nearby, he would not have heard a rustle from the rescuers as they passed.

When they had completed their detour of the town, Broken Trail took over the lead. The place where he had left Spotted Dog was only a short way ahead. His throat felt tight as they drew near. What if Spotted Dog was dead? What if his body had been lying under the juniper's branches for days, exposed to the elements and unprotected from scavengers?

And then they came upon him, not lying under the juniper but sitting with his back against the trunk of the cedar tree, his splinted leg stretched out in front of him. His head hung to one side, and his eyes were shut.

Walks Crooked approached his son, knelt beside him, and gently touched his shoulder.

"Ho! Spotted Dog," he said softly, "we have come to take you home."

Spotted Dog opened his eyes.

"What?" His voice was faint.

"Swift Fox and Broken Trail are with me. We have come to take you home."

Spotted Dog's face looked tired and ill. His bloodshot eyes seemed to have receded into their sockets, and his skin had an ashy hue. He whimpered, "Many days and nights passed while I waited. I was cold. I thought Broken Trail had left me here to die."

"Why did you think that? I gave my word," Broken Trail protested.

Walks Crooked examined Spotted Dog's left leg, seeing how it was bound with poles and packed with moss.

"Did Broken Trail set your leg? It is well done. Now we'll make a litter to carry you to the river, where Black Elk waits with our canoes. By tomorrow morning you will be home. With warmth, food and rest, you will soon be well."

Spotted Dog shook his head. "Too late. At first I was afraid. But no longer. After three days and three nights of hiding under those branches, I wanted to see the sky. My spirit is ready for its journey to the Land without Trouble."

"Do not speak of dying," Walks Crooked said. "You will live to become a great warrior."

Broken Trail stepped aside, his spirit troubled. Had he travelled so hard, brought the others all this way, only to see Spotted Dog die? After so much effort, he could not bear the thought that it would end in failure.

Spotted Dog grunted. "Me a great warrior? You say the thing that is not. It was my foot that broke the branch when we crept up on the sentry. I caused Hunting Hawk's death. Because of me, the war party failed. I am unworthy to be Walks Crooked's son."

"You are young. Your leg will heal. There will be more war parties. You will take many scalps."

"Whether I live or die, I'll never be a warrior."

Walks Crooked placed his hand on his son's forehead. "Your skin is hot. When we reach home, Wolf Woman will give you a healing drink, and we'll put you in the sweat lodge to drive out your fever. As soon as your health is restored, your fighting spirit will return."

Did Walks Crooked believe his own words? His voice was weary, and he looked old. Soon there would be no more war parties for him. On his face was the sadness of a man whose dreams can never come true.

Spotted Dog looked into his father's eyes. "There is something that I must tell you," he whispered hoarsely.

"Not now." Walks Crooked said gently. He held his son's hand. "You must rest."

"I must tell you. I am ready to tell the truth . . . ," the boy took a great, shuddering breath, "about the golden eagle—"

"No!" Broken Trail shouted. Whether Spotted Dog lived or died, this secret must not be told. "Save your strength! Let me tell them what you told me."

All eyes turned to Broken Trail, who glared at Spotted Dog, forbidding him to contradict.

"Spotted Dog told me everything about the golden eagle. He told me how it came to him with a noise like a thunderclap—shooting from the sun with a lightning bolt in its talons." He hesitated. What was next? Yes! He remembered.

"The eagle spoke from above as it circled the spot where Spotted Dog waited. It said to him, 'Do not fear. I shall never desert you. You will be safe in the shadow of my wings.'"

He sneaked a sideways glance at Spotted Dog, who looked up at him, speechless.

"Then the golden eagle circled upwards, making wider and wider circles in the sky until it disappeared." As he spoke, Broken Trail's upraised arm traced the spiralling flight of the fabulous bird. He was sweating as he finished. "This was Spotted Dog's true dream, as he told it to me." Broken Trail lowered his arm.

No one spoke. Walks Crooked looked astonished. "My son told you all this? It is more than he revealed to the council of warriors."

Broken Trail turned again to Spotted Dog, to warn him not to contradict. But Spotted Dog was not looking at him. His eyes glowed. With a terrible effort he pulled free the hand that his father was holding and pointed to the sky, pointed to the sun that was now declining in the west.

"Look! Look! The golden eagle!"

Broken Trail shivered. Suddenly he felt a mystic presence. But when he stared in the direction that Spotted Dog pointed, all he saw was the glare of the sun.

"I am ready!" Spotted Dog called out, his voice strong and clear. On his face was an expression of wonder and joy. "Try me!" he shouted at the sun. "I can be worthy!"

Then his arm dropped across his chest. His eyes closed.

"No!" Walks Crooked cried out.

It was over. The rescue had failed. Spotted Dog had set forth on his journey to the Land without Trouble. Overcome by grief and disappointment, Broken Trail lowered his face.

Suddenly Swift Fox's voice broke the silence. "Look there! He's breathing!"

Broken Trail lifted his eyes and saw Spotted Dog's chest moving up and down. Death had not claimed him: he was in a trance.

Walks Crooked raised his head and looked directly at Broken Trail. "Spotted Dog told you things about his vision that he never before revealed to anyone. And now he has seen it a second time. It is a wondrous thing for a warrior to receive his vision twice. Surely my son is destined for greatness." The look on his face was radiant and yet soft, as if he had dreamed some great happiness and awoke to find it true.

All at once Broken Trail was very happy, and he felt an unexpected kinship with Spotted Dog. Those long days alone in the forest, cold and hungry, had been Spotted Dog's true vigil. They had brought him to the brink. Broken Trail's words, borrowed from Young Bear, had done the rest.

Only Broken Trail knew that Spotted Dog had never seen his *oki* before.

The Great Spirit hated a lie. But would he not forgive a falsehood whose only purpose was to spare a loving father pain and to give the son a chance to make a new start? In a way, the Great Spirit himself had transformed the lie into truth, for there was no fakery in what they had witnessed. Only the Great Spirit could have sent such a vision. Everyone present could see its power.

Walks Crooked tucked a blanket around his son and sat by his side. It seemed that the exhausted boy had slipped from his trance into quiet sleep.

Broken Trail and Swift Fox stood on either side, facing each other. Their eyes met.

"We're in danger here," said Swift Fox. "It's fortunate for us that no one from the Mississauga village happened to be near."

Before he could answer, Broken Trail's nose suddenly caught the scent of wolverine. Looking about, he saw nothing. Yet there was no mistaking that pungent musk. Swift Fox gave no sign of noticing it. Perhaps it was meant for Broken Trail alone.

"We must hurry," he agreed. "It is not safe to linger."

Together they fashioned a litter out of poles and twisted vines. Then they shouldered the litter and carried Spotted Dog through the forest to the canoes. Spotted Dog was still asleep when they lowered him gently into Walks Crooked and Black Elk's canoe.

Everything has changed, Broken Trail thought as they paddled down the river. A new beginning for Spotted Dog. A new beginning for himself.

Walks Crooked was his enemy no longer. He, Broken Trail,

had proved his worthiness to be a warrior. Now it was time to prepare himself for the real work of his life. What lay before him he still did not know. But he had taken the first step, and that was how every journey began.

All the way to the Oneida village, Spotted Dog slept, warm under blankets and rocked by the motion of the canoe. A snow flurry blew from the west. Helped by wind and current, the canoes reached home just before dawn.

Spotted Dog did not wake up until the canoe touched the riverbank. As he was being lifted onto the shore, he turned his face toward Broken Trail.

"You saved my life."

No one else would ever know exactly and completely what he meant.

After Spotted Dog had been carried to Wolf Woman's lodge, Broken Trail turned his steps toward the Bear Clan longhouse. At the entrance he stopped, suddenly realizing that he did not want to go in just yet. The sun had not risen. Everyone would still be asleep, but as soon as anyone saw him, the longhouse would come to life. He was not ready to cope with a crush of people, even those dear to him, or to answer the questions they would ask. And so he drew back at the last moment.

He made his way slowly through the fields, between planting mounds stripped of the last fruits of harvest. Scarcely noticing his surroundings, he entered the forest, which was still shadowy in the dawning light.

As he walked, he found his mind turning to the day that had changed the course of his life, the tenth day of his spirit quest, and to the moment that his mystic vision had been snatched from him. He had not been ready for his vision, he thought. It was right for the unseen spirits to have kept him waiting until he learned who he was and what he was.

He supposed that the first glimmering had come at his blackest moment, when his warning to the soldiers at Kings Mountain had gained him only ridicule, and he had feared Elijah had been brutally killed. A sign had come in a beam of light piercing the darkness of the washout cavity under the maple tree. He remembered moving his hand so that the bright spot would fall upon his skin. As he watched the tiny beam of light waver in the darkness, he had for the first time experienced the feeling that the Great Spirit had a special plan for his life.

As he and Elijah travelled north together, Elijah had tried to make him see that he belonged both to the world into which he had been born and to the world that had adopted him.

What once had seemed a fault that he must struggle to overcome he saw now as a gift that he might use to help the native people. He was not, as he had sometimes feared, stranded in a no man's land between two worlds. Nor was he forced to choose between the one and the other. Instead, he could be a bridge to connect them. Through the power given to him, his thoughts could soar above all the warring nations, white and native. Their strife seemed never-ending. And yet, he thought, the Sun our Father and the Moon our Mother shone on all alike. This great earth, with its mountains and valleys, its forests, lakes and rivers, was vast enough for all to share.

Elijah would be at his side, finding the path that was right for him. It was neither the path of a Loyalist soldier nor the path of a hunter-warrior. Saved from the battlefield for some greater purpose, somehow, somewhere, Elijah would join him in his work so that the tragedy of the Cherokees need not be repeated over and over again.

He stopped walking, and for a few moments gazed along the path that he had taken with Young Bear the day he killed the elk. He stood absolutely still, listening to the murmur of wind in the trees and smelling the scent of pine. A crow cawed, the forest's rough voice waking him to where he was. Broken Trail became aware that he was cold. Now he wanted to be with people whom he loved. He wanted their nearness and their warmth. His heart felt light as he started back.

Two days later, Broken Trail joined the council of warriors. When the pipe passed around the circle, he too inhaled the sharp, bitter smoke. While others spoke of his bravery, he did not allow himself a ghost of a smile. But it was sweet to hear Walks Crooked's words of praise.

After the council meeting, he strolled with his uncle down to the river. Hard grains of blowing snow stung their faces as they walked along the shore.

"I would make a feast in your honour," Carries a Quiver said. "But how can we feast at this time of sorrow? Five warriors dead."

"I don't want a feast. It is better that we hunt to build up our stores of food."

"I shall hunt with you." Carries a Quiver paused. "It is time you had a rifle."

"For a long time, I've been thinking the same thing."

"Let us go back to the longhouse. I have a rifle to give you, now that you are a man. It belonged to your father. I have saved it for you ever since he died at Barren Hill."

"I shall try to be worthy of it."

"You already are."

Broken Trail listened to the sound of the wind as he walked at Carries a Quiver's side. It blew from the west, from beyond the great lakes, from lands that he had never seen, although someday he would. But first he must make himself ready for the long trail of his life.

"Uncle," he said, "when my turn comes to speak to the council of warriors, I shall urge that we make peace with the Mississaugas. I shall say that the time has come to put a stop to raids against our brothers."

"Then you and I shall speak with one voice to the council. Finally, others may be willing to see the need to find a better way. The world for which I prepared you will soon be no more. As the world changes, we must change, too."

What lies ahead? Broken Trail wondered. Something better? Something worse? He supposed that the future would be better for the colonists but worse for the native people. But he could help them, moving back and forth, being part of both. *Mitakue`oyasin*, he thought. We are all related.

They had reached the dancing circle when Carries a Quiver stopped and laid his hand upon Broken Trail's shoulder. Startled, Broken Trail turned to him.

"Remember your first deer?" Carries a Quiver asked.

"Does any hunter forget his first deer? Uncle, you stood at this spot and made the boast."

"I called you a hunter who brings meat for the people."

"I remember the scowl on Walks Crooked's face."

"And now there is no one who speaks more highly in your praise."

Broken Trail felt a rush of happiness, like a spring of fresh water welling up inside. He threw back his head and laughed.

Carries a Quiver's solemn face cracked in a smile. And then he was laughing too.

ABOUT THE AUTHOR

Jean Rae Baxter was born in Toronto, grew up in Hamilton, and lived for many years in the Kingston area. During her career as a secondary school English teacher, she wrote articles, poems and short plays. It was after retiring that she first turned her hand to writing fiction, soon discovering that this was what she liked to do best. She writes for adults and for young people. Her first book, *A Twist of Malice*, was a collection of short stories, published in 2005. It was followed by her young adult novel, *The Way Lies North*, in 2007. This novel received the 2008 Arts Hamilton Award for a young adult book and was nominated for the 2009 Red Maple Award in the Ontario Library Association's Forest of Reading Program and for the 2010 Stellar, British Columbia's teen readers' choice award. *The Way Lies North* tells the story of fifteen-year-old Charlotte Hooper, driven from her home and separated from her sweetheart by the violence of the American Revolution.

Jean Rae Baxter's next novel, *Looking for Cardenio*, a literary murder mystery published in 2008, imagines what might happen if somebody discovered a manuscript of Shakespeare's lost play.

With *Broken Trail*, she returns to the time of the American Revolution in a story about two teenage brothers, one a runaway who spends three years living as an Oneida while the other serves as a soldier. She is now working on a third novel involving the same characters featured in *The Way Lies North* and *Broken Trail.*

When she is not writing, she enjoys the company of family and friends—her Scottish terrier Robbie being part of both. Her favourite activities are reading and travel. She lives in Hamilton, Ontario, where she helps to organize the LiT LiVe reading series and serves on the Arts Hamilton Literary Advisory Committee. Visit her website at www.jeanraebaxter.ca.

Marquis Book Printing Inc.

Québec, Canada
2010

Printed on Silva Enviro 100% post-consumer EcoLogo certified paper, processed chlorine free and manufactured using biogas energy.